MW01690690

CHARGE IT TO THE GAME 2

Charge it to the Game 2

Tammy's Story

KEAIDY BENNETT

LEXXIKHAN PRESENTS
PUBLISHING

LexxiKhan Presents Publishing

Disclaimer:
The story presented herein addresses serious topics, but it does not glorify the sale of drugs or criminal behavior. Instead, it aims to prompt readers to contemplate the harsh realities and consequences of engaging in "the Game."

This book contains an excerpt from the next installment in the Charge It to the Game series. It may be edited or deleted prior to actual publication.

This book was previously published under the name Keaidy Selmon.

978-1-958335-03-1

For the Afro-Latina who feels like she doesn't fit in:
We're enjoying our own lane, now.

xo

OTHER BOOKS BY KEAIDY BENNETT

Charge it to the Game

Charge it to the Game 3: Three Sides to Every Story

Charge it to the Game 4: Pride Comes B4 Destruction (Coming 2023)

Somewhere Between Love & Misunderstanding

The Chronicles of a Love Addict

When a Woman's Fed Up (Coming 2023)

She Fell in Love With a Boss

Shut Up & Finish Your Book Already

JOIN THE CLUB

Join our mailing list today! Just text **BOOKTRAP** to **407-890-8882**.
Want more information on how to publish your own story?
Text **WeReady** to **407-890-8882**.

| 1 |

How Dare She?

2013

Kyle Cole sat in his new, spacious, and lonely condo, thinking about the one thing he had been trying so desperately to forget – Tamia Santiago.

It had been four months since she decided to leave him and the life they shared, but the pain he still felt made the breakup feel like it had just happened yesterday.

When she packed up and left, she didn't even have the decency to tell him she was leaving to his face. Instead, she wrote him a short and sweet letter and took nothing but the clothes on her back before he made it home in the morning like he told her he would.

Since she had been gone, all of their communication was brief. When he was finally able to get a hold of her, thanks to a number he got through her old bank job, he called her twice to check up on her. She had retired from the street life and was no longer getting financial support from anyone else, so she found out just how tough life really was. He had never told her that he had a secret stash put away in case of emergencies, and he had sent more than half of the $60,000 he had saved away to help get her back on her feet.

He knew it was only a matter of time before he became stronger than he was, so he didn't think twice about sending her so much.

He grabbed the letter she left him and battled the decision to re-read her words one last time. Her penmanship was impeccable, and the letter still smelt like her favorite perfume.

Suddenly, there was a gentle knock at his door. K.Y took it to be one of his boys and decided to just let the knock go unanswered, but then the gentle taps became louder and louder.

"Whatever you have, I don't want it," he screamed out.

Once he responded, and the person on the other side of the door knew he was home, their knocks became more incessant.

K.Y. finally decided to go to the door to find out who it was. When he looked through the peephole, the woman on the other end seemed very familiar. Still, he just couldn't remember where he had seen this beautiful woman from before. As much as he did not want company, his curiosity had to figure out who this woman was.

The striking and well-shaped woman immediately walked in the moment he opened the door.

"I'm sorry but do I know you," K.Y asked. He didn't even bother to hide his aggravation of this stranger just inviting herself into his home.

"I guess it is a little weird to see me fully clothed," she chuckled. "The last time we met, the only thing you saw me in was my red bottoms."

"Mrs. Carter," he asked to make sure that he had correctly identified the name with the face.

"Please just call me Josie. I'm glad I didn't have to go through the full demonstration to make sure you remembered," she replied seductively.

The thought of this gorgeous woman standing in his home naked made K.Y hard.

"From the looks of what is going on in those basketball shorts, I guess you wish you would have just waited for it," she giggled. "If you play your cards right, we might still be able to make that happen."

K.Y became embarrassed that the woman knew how excited she had just made him. It had been months since he felt the warm embrace of a woman sexually. There was no possible way to be discreet about his current erection.

"I hope you don't take this the wrong way, but why are you here? I met you once two years ago, and I never saw you again after that. What made you come check me out now," he asked.

"You and I share a common interest in a mutual friend. I want her."

The thought of Tammy instantly caused him to go soft. Although this woman was his type, she could never be the woman that he was still in love with.

"Well, as you can see, she is no longer here. You're too late," Kyle grumbled as he finally took a seat on his comfortable leather lazy boy recliner.

"I gave you some time before I came over here because I expected you to be over her by now, but it's obvious that you are not." She replied before walking over to his couch and taking a seat herself.

"Well, she's a single woman now, so she's all yours. I still don't understand why you would come bothering me for a woman that is no longer mine anymore."

"Contrary to your belief, she is not a single woman, and that is exactly why I'm here. When she was here with you, she was not a threat to me and my relationship. Now that she is no longer with you, I have a huge problem on my hands."

K.Y was instantly confused. He had worked desperately for almost a year to get the attention of Tammy, and he knew that with the love they had shared, there is no way she would just run off and be with someone else already.

"Look, lady, I have no idea what you're talking about, and I don't care to find out about your problems. Now, if you don't mind, I would appreciate it if you would get out of my house."

"Aw. I know going through a breakup is not easy, but if you were smart enough, you would have figured out by now that Tammy was not only a problem for me," she declared. "I really thought you would have figured out by now the kind of person you had been dealing with all of this time."

"I don't know what your issue is with her, and I don't care to know. If you insist on staying in my house, then the least you can do is show the woman some respect. The moment you try to play her again, you are out of here," he growled.

The woman instantly began laughing so hard that you could see tears falling from her eyes. "Please stop. Your jokes are so amusing. I can't handle it anymore," she replied while trying to catch her breath from laughing. "I understand that love is blind, and you are young, but you can't possibly be as stupid as you are making yourself appear at this moment." Josie took a few moments to pull herself together before she was able to continue. "I really do not mean to be so rude, but I just assumed I would be walking into a whole different situation. Sadly, the woman you are still in love with is not who you think she is at all. She played me, but she undoubtedly played the hell out of you."

"How the hell do you figure that? You don't know a damn thing about me."

"I do know that when you two met, you were running shit down here in Orlando. Now, look at you; instead of being out to get your revenge, you are moping around foolishly in this apartment."

"Look, we all have to take a loss to be a boss. I took some losses, but things are not over for me. She didn't leave me high and dry. I understand why things wouldn't have worked out. She wanted to go legit, and who am I to stop her."

"Please don't cause me to start cracking up in here. That girl hasn't been legit in years, and there is no turning back for her now. You've been doing your thing all this time, so do you honestly think you could ever be 100% legit ever again?"

"No, I don't, but she and I are two different people. That's the reason why we couldn't be together. I love this game, and I can never give it up. She's been in the street life all of her life, and now she's tired of it. She doesn't want to lose anyone else she loves to these streets, so she made the decision to go her separate way."

"Wow! I always knew that girl was a good ass actress, but I had no idea just how good she was. She hasn't been in the streets all of her life. She grew up in the suburbs, for crying out loud."

"I don't believe you and a single thing you're saying. I knew that woman for over a year and a half, and she let me get to know her in ways that she didn't even let her family get to know. I don't want to get nasty with you, but I will if I have to. Please excuse yourself before I get to that point."

"In your eyes, she was a huge-time drug dealer, but did you ever see her handle the product herself? Besides the sale she did with me, did you ever see her make that kind of money that fast ever again?"

K.Y didn't want to believe anything this woman was saying. It took him so long to get to know her, and he knew the kind of woman Tamia was. She seemed legit, and there was no way he could allow this woman to drag her name through the mud any longer.

"Get the fuck out. You don't know what you're even talking about. You come in my house dressed like the whore you are, and you just couldn't wait for Tamia to leave so you could try to sew your oats over here too."

"Please don't flatter yourself. I'll get out, but you know deep down there is a part of you that is curious to find out if what I'm saying is true. Put on your shirt and shoes and come with me."

K.Y had enough of taking orders from people, and Tamia was the only woman he ever allowed to tell him what to do.

"I'm not doing shit unless you learn how to talk to me properly. You came over here, so you must need my help for whatever you're trying to do. Learn some respect and how to talk to a man when you're dealing with me. Now ask me nicely," he said sternly.

"The last time I met you, I couldn't get you to say a word. I have to admit that this side of you is rather is sexy," Josie said while running her hands down her thick thighs. "Can you please get ready and come with me," she asked nicely.

"That's better. Go to your car and wait for me; I'll be down in 10 minutes."

"I don't have that kind of time, so if you're coming with me, then you need to come now."

"What the hell did I just say to you? Take your ass downstairs and wait. If you can't wait, then leave. If you leave, then forget you know me and my address and never bring your ass over here again."

For a year and a half, K.Y had been used to taking orders, so it felt good to be in charge of everything again.

"I'll be right in front of the building. Please do not take too long because we are on a time limit, and I don't want you to miss your shot at a chance of the truth," she said, sounding very sincere.

K.Y. didn't need 10 minutes, but he didn't want to let her feel like she had any control over him. He put on his shirt, jeans, a light jacket to protect him from the brisk January air, shoes, and grabbed his piece before locking up and heading downstairs. Just as she said she would, Josie sat right in front of the building in her all-black 2013 Audi S6

K.Y couldn't lie, this chick was fine, but he didn't like the way she was dealing with him. She had to be at least 5'5without her heels on. She had a beautiful light honey complexion but was built like a video model, so it left him to wonder what her ethnicity was. Her caramel brown hair was long and flowed all the way down to the middle of her back. Her hands were the only sign that this woman was a little older, but she still looked better than most women half of her age.

"If she's so bad, then what do you want with her, and how long have you supposedly known all of this," he asked once he was settled into the vehicle.

"I've known her for years, and we haven't always seen eye to eye. We ran in a similar circle a few years ago, so it made doing business impossible at one point. We agreed to make a truce three years ago, which is why I didn't think anything of it the time she came by my business. She knew that if anyone could help her get rid of her product fast, it would be me."

"I still don't understand what your problem with her is."

"My children's father and I dated for 9 years. I really thought that we were going to get married, but then Tammy came along. He and I had been separated for a really long time, and they had already had a bit of history. They began spending more time together, and he began spending less time at home with the children and me. I really thought he would just get over our issues, and things would go back to normal, but you can't always help who you love. I thought helping her out would get her out of my life for good. Instead, it helped solidify her position in his life," her voice began to crack, and it became evident that she was holding back tears. "She lied to you and to me just get what she wanted. Why do they get to have it all while we live alone with the pain?"

K.Y. sat silently for the rest of the car ride. He couldn't believe everything that she was saying, and it was beginning to be a little overwhelming.

After driving for what felt like forever, they finally pulled in front of a building that he knew all too well.

"How is bringing me to Tammy's old apartment really helping to prove your point? I've been here plenty of times already, and this place is not new to me. It would only surprise me to find out that she was still living here when she told me she moved back home."

"Please just follow me. I promise if you go upstairs with an open mind, you will find out soon enough that she isn't as trustworthy as she led you to believe."

They walked up the two flights of stairs to the third-floor apartment that K.Y had been to many times before. Josie took her car keys, and to his surprise, opened up the apartment door that once belonged to the women he loved.

They walked inside, and everything that he remembered was in its exact place.

"I don't get it. I thought she got rid of this place when she and I moved into our condo together."

"This place was never hers to give up. I allowed her to stay here for about a year. She paid me rent, and I let her have free reign of the place because I was always out of town on business."

Why woul• she lie to me about where she live•? K.Y thought to himself.

Josie walked over to the over sized chair by the window that he and Tammy had countless intimate conversations. She lit a spliff and made herself comfy on the leather chair.

"She lied to me about where she lived, and I don't understand why, but this still doesn't prove your point about her being a terrible person."

"Why would she need to lie to the man she loved about the place she called home. You guys loved each other, right? So wouldn't you need to know where to be able to locate your woman if she was ever in some sort of danger or trouble?"

"I get where you are going with this, but her father also made sure that she was well taken care of out here."

Josie sat up and looked at K.Y with a puzzled look on her face. "Now I wonder how a dead man can manage to take such good care of his little girl from his grave."

"I can assure you that he is not dead. She communicated with him weekly, and she even had a family friend vouch for her. So please find a different angle."

"Delino Santiago died four years ago," she said as she walked over to her computer table. She dug through a few files before finally finding the document she was looking for. She handed him an obituary that seemed to prove everything that she was saying about Tammy's father. Josie handed him another photo that showed Mr. Santiago in his casket with Tammy at the podium next to it.

"Then why would she have a contact under her phone as 'Papi'? One of her family friends was very protective over her because he said that he promised her father he would look out for her and keep her safe."

"Jason promised him that four years ago while Mr. Santiago was on his death bed. I had no idea why their bond was so close, but I always tried to be understanding to it, hoping that he would see that no matter what, I would love him and would be there."

"This doesn't make sense. He made it seem like this man was still alive."

"I'm not sure why he would have done that to you, but I can assure you that Delino Santiago is dead. Tee is Hispanic and we sometimes tend to call our men 'papi', so that could explain the contact in her phone. I can promise you that they have been involved together for at least 5 years. I use to have a picture of the two of them together at his funeral before I learned that they were an item and destroyed the image," she said. "He kept a contact in his phone as 'princess,' and I always thought that was for our eldest daughter, but it was for her. I really thought that man was not capable of knowing what love really was, but he's treated her so much different than I've seen him act with any woman before."

K.Y paced back and forth while he tried to go over all of the information that Josie had just given him. "You're a hating bitch, and you haven't shown me anything that really verifies anything you've said. I never met her father, so I don't know what the man looks like, and this could be fake," he said, throwing the obituary back at her. "Now hurry up and take me home before I snap and say something I'll later regret."

Josie got up from her chair and walked over to the clearly hurt K.Y.

"I know this is a lot of information, and your love for her makes everything I'm telling you hard to believe, but I need you to trust me." She grabbed his arm and led him over to the same chair she was just sitting in. Then, she guided him down into the seat and gently sat on top of him. "I don't have any reason to lie to you. Even though I was instantly attracted to the both of you, I stayed away because I sincerely wanted the two of you to work. I could tell that you loved her even from that one meeting we had. I really thought she felt the same way because you were the first person in her personal camp that I ever met. I've heard many things about you from doing my research on you first, and I know that you didn't deserve the treatment you got. I just need you to be patient with me, and I promise you that I can show you everything better than I can tell you. A man like you deserves so much more than you received, and you should at least know the truth about the woman that deceived you into falling in love with her."

After all of this time, what would this woman get for lying to me? Kyle thought to himself as he began to find comfort in her touch. He wanted to doubt everything that was coming out of her mouth, but he wouldn't be honest with himself if he didn't admit that he had already had some doubts about Tammy. For example, he spent many sleepless nights wondering why she refused to allow him to meet the man that seemed to be so important to her. In fact, it had been the start of a few arguments.

***

"It just doesn't make sense to me is what I'm getting at! You say you love me and you're wearing the ring I gave you, so why can't I meet the man? I wanted to do things the proper way by asking for your hand in marriage before proposing to you, but you wouldn't even let me do that," Kyle yelled out to Tammy.

"I don't know who the fuck you think you're screaming at, but you better lower your tone before I really get upset. You asked a simple question, and I provided a simple answer – no! You just have to trust me that it's just not a good idea. If I were just one of your birds that you were used to, that would have worked, but you'll honestly be doing way more harm than good," Tammy replied.

"I'm going to have to meet him eventually, so I don't get why I can't do it ahead of time. I'm a grown-ass man, and I can handle anything that some guy throws at me."

"That's really cute, but I promise you that you have no idea who you are dealing with. If my old man was just some regular guy, then I would have set this meeting up a long time ago, but I can promise you that he's not. I already know that the moment he knew what was going on, the wedding would immediately be off.

I love him, and I refuse to be defiant on his wishes, and I know he wouldn't want me to get married. It's just that easy."

"So then what are you going to tell him once it actually happens," he asked her.

"*If* we get married, he would have no choice but to accept it.

He and I are a lot alike in certain ways. Once we've made up our minds and followed through with something, we understand that there is no point in trying to persuade the other person into our personal views. If I go to him an unmarried woman, he will see to it that it stays that way.

When I was little, my father used to tell me that all men were dogs and not to be foolish enough to fall for their lies. It's a miracle I'm even considering walking down the aisle and being a bride despite all I've seen and heard, so please don't push it any further. You asked a question, and I gave you an answer. Now, please leave me the hell alone."

***

Josie handed him the spliff that she had been smoking and offered him something to drink.

"Nah, I don't think that will be a good idea. I really just need a clear mind to sort through all of this. Part of me believes some of what you're saying, but there is a huge part of me that feels like that woman was nothing but honest to me. We never hid anything from each other, no matter how much the truth would hurt. That's the shit I liked the most about shawty. She kept everything a hundred since day one."

"So you mean to tell me that you never once questioned any of those robberies you experienced while dealing with her?

From what I heard about you in the streets, that shit was so uncommon before that chick came around. You never once believed that she might have been the one setting you up all along?"

"I never once thought that. I got involved in this shit early, and she proved to me that I didn't know the game as well as I thought I did. Thanks to her, I started making some big power moves, and a lot of my business deals were smarter than they had been previously. She taught me how to rule my camp with an iron fist and even warned me ahead of time that big results would come with enormous consequences.

Once I started really making things happen, I already knew I would have to deal with some haters. Before her, I had taken losses, but she taught me how to bounce back. There were plenty of times I had thought about getting revenge on a few people, and she actually helped me follow through on a few. Then, there were certain situations when she showed me the value of just 'charging it to the game.' You win some, and you lose some, but the object of the game is to come out on top and alive. Some battles just weren't worth fighting because I realized the risks that were involved.

That woman helped me out way too much for me to really believe that she would have been setting me up at all. She was about her money, and so was I; we were a team. Why would she have a hand in the downfall of our empire together?"

Josie was hesitant to begin speaking. It was evident to anyone that heard him talk about Tee that he had clearly placed her on a pedestal.

She placed her arm around his neck and used the other hand to caress his chest. "You're right about her being about her money, but I'm sad to say that the team she was trying to build an empire with was not with you. Unfortunately, you were just a pawn who got caught up in her game of trying to make it to the top. I've watched her hustle and manipulate situations and people before. I just never thought she would do something as sneaky as this.

She used the fact that you were young and inexperienced to her benefit. You fell in love with her, which made you blind to her tricks. A real ride or die would have held you down until the very end. That woman bounced the moment things became too tough, so there was no way she was really down for you.

She knew you were a part of this kind of lifestyle when she met you, and she continued to deal with you. Then, your organization is built up and takes your largest loss ever, and then she bounces. You can't be that in love that you won't clearly see that she had a hand in your downfall."

He handed her back the spliff.

"I know that it looks bad, but she was good to me, and that is how I'll always remember her."

"I just can't believe that a woman who loved you half as much as you loved her had the heart to look you in those beautiful eyes and end your relationship. Didn't she understand the magnitude of all of the losses you've experienced in life?"

"She didn't," he replied. "She left me a letter and was gone before I had a chance to tell her she was making a mistake. She said she knew if she told it to my face, she wouldn't be able to go through with it.

I know how she is, though, and she already made up her mind and went through with her decision, so now there is no point in fighting. I just have to love her from afar."

"How dare she? She couldn't even give you a chance to try to win her heart back, but she expects you to believe that she actually loved you? The time that you two shared wasn't even worth the decency to say goodbye to your face. At least she has the decency to leave and stay gone. It would be a problem if she was still calling or accepting your calls."

K.Y couldn't hide his facial expression. Even though they didn't talk as much as he would have liked, they have had a few conversations.

"I take it by your reaction that there is some kind of communication. Well, at least your smart enough not to give her any money if she asks for it or tell her how much you have."

His silence and uneasiness confirmed to her that he was doing the exact opposite.

"This is even worst than I thought. Kyle, you have to accept the facts; she set you up. She taught you more of the game than she was supposed to and realizes that you can bounce back on your feet with the information she gave you. She is smart enough to distance herself but wise enough not to cut you off so that she can come back around and hit you up whenever you get back on your feet again. I can't believe how conniving she is."

K.Y. instantly thought back to their last conversation. Tammy was grateful for the money she sent him, but she almost seemed angry that he had withheld so much money and information from her.

***

"Kyle Cole, where the hell did you get that kind of money to be able to send it to me," Tammy asked him.

"It doesn't matter, baby. You needed it, and I had it, so you know if I have it and you need it, then it's yours," he replied, meaning every word of it.

"I just don't get it. I only needed a few dollars to make it through the month; I really didn't need over $30,000. What doesn't make sense to me is that either you are back on and started making big moves again, or you were holding back some big secrets from me when we were together. What's up? Which one is it?"

K.Y. was a little nervous to respond because he didn't expect her to react like this. "I had a few dollars put away, and I dipped into it so that you and I could be straight. I know how you feel about me being back in these streets, but I don't know any other way to survive. I was willing to try to learn with you, but you bounced, so now I'm just going to go back to what I know."

"How do you forget to tell your woman that you have that kind of money stashed somewhere? I can get 5 or 10 stacks because that's something light, but you had enough to send me 30 stacks and still have money in your pocket. That's part of the reason why we are not together now.

It's not just about you being in these streets, but you started holding secrets, and that's the kind of shit I don't like," Tammy replied. "I appreciate the money and the help you've been giving me all of this time, but I should have known taking your call was a mistake. It's hard enough to try to piece my life together and move on without finding out that it's going to be so easy for you to make moves and move on without me. I guess I always felt needed when we were together, and this just kind of showed me that you didn't need me as much as I thought you did."

"I never needed you, shawty. I love you, and there is a big difference. That love makes me want to keep you around. I'm always going to be grateful for the help and information that you've given me. Still, I'm confident in my ability to bounce back."

"I never doubted your ability to bounce back. I knew you'd be back on your feet in no time. They forgot about you on those blocks in Orlando, and it's time that you remind them what you're capable of and who they are dealing with. Even though we can't be together like that, I will always be here and be around to talk to you."

"Maybe when I'm back on, it will convince you enough to come back home where you belong."

"I didn't bounce because you're not on anymore. I bounced because the streets are your first love, and I'll always be second to that. I'm tired of the street life, and I just want normalcy. Maybe one day you'll want the same, and if I'm still around and available, then we can try to cross that bridge when we get there. But for now, we just want and need two different things out of life."

"I want normalcy too. We can achieve it together. Let's just do it. I'll get out for good, and I'll go legit."

"How can you really expect two broke people to go legit? I'm still a struggling college student, and you just sent me most of the money you had put away."

"I have another 28 stacks put away," he said. "We can use that money to help build up your business and this time be 100% legit. I'll get a job, and you can finish school."

"That sounds cute, and if I really felt like that was attainable, I would have suggested that before I left. You have expensive taste, and so do I. We're both young and don't have to rush into anything. This space can be good for us to work on ourselves, and it can help bring us closer together.

You build your empire how you want to, and I do the same from my end. If we are meant to be together, then that is precisely what will happen in the end. In the meantime, you do what you need to so that you can be good, and I'll do the same."

"I just don't get it. I'm doing everything that I think I can to get us to work, and it seems like you are giving me every excuse as to why it can't work."

"Cut the bullshit K.Y. These are not excuses. You have always been the dreamer, and I have always been the realist of our team. How will we ever be able to survive, much less plan a wedding or family, if neither one of us is on our feet?

I'm almost finished with school, and I am possibly up for a huge promotion, so I have my life together. You want me to believe that at the age of 25, you are going to give up the only hustle that you have ever really known to tag along on my business? I would have to see some serious effort from you first.

I helped you bring your empire to where it was. All the while, I was urging you to do something smart with your money or to at least invest it in a business so you wouldn't be where you are today, and you didn't do anything like that. I told you in the very beginning that I thought you were hard-headed, and the fact that you are where you are proves that to me," Tammy replied.

"When I took that leap of faith to go with you and make it known to my family, I took the risk of being cut off completely by my old man, and that was precisely what happened. I used to have thousands of dollars coming in from him monthly just because I was doing what I was supposed to be doing, and I gave all of that up just to be with you all the time. I was determined to make us work, which is why I stayed on your ass as much as I did. When you thought I was just nagging, I was doing my best to make sure that we didn't end up here.

You were stubborn, secretive, and downright sneaky at the end of the relationship, so I left. I need to see some major improvements from you before I can even think about getting back with you. Much less moving my entire life back down to Florida," she paused and softened her tone before continuing. "You think this is easy on me, but it's not. I don't have you, and now I'm back home trying to prove myself to my old man, and it's turning out to be much harder than I would have ever expected. I feel alone most of the time, and the stress of not having the same lifestyle I had before is really pissing me off.

It's hard, but you know exactly what you need to do if you want me back. If I'm not worth it to you, you can just move on and go back to doing what you've spent most of your life doing. The game is not going to be good to you forever, which is why it's always best to leave the bitch while you're still in her good graces. Whenever you get your life together, you know how to reach me," and without another word, she disconnected the call.

***

Josie took her hand and gently brought Kyle's down to her over-endowed breasts.

"It's not easy to get over a first love. It's even harder when you begin to doubt if that person was real to you or if you fell in love with an illusion of who you wanted that person to be." Josie said as she used her manicured fingers to caress his ear.

"I'm at least twice your age, and it still pains me to know the horrible truth. But I couldn't sit back and do nothing while Tammy got away with breaking your heart and continuing the cycle by keeping you on a short leash. I've been there with my ex, and it's clear that he taught her his same tricks because she is now using them on you.

If you ever need anyone to talk to, I'm here for you. We can get through this together instead of suffering silently alone," she said, sounding so sincere. "Just give me a little time to get together all the proof and evidence you need. You'll see that I'm being for real in everything I'm saying to you.

I know it's hard to let an hour of information from a stranger change your mind about a love that took you years to build, but I promise you that soon you will see what I'm talking about. The woman you fell in love with is a self-centered, manipulating, egotistical, and conniving woman. She planned for you to fall in love with her so that you would never be able to suspect what she has planned next."

| 2 |

Get Angry MotherF*cker

Tamia Santiago was born in the middle of the '80s when crack was being sold and done heavily in the streets she lived on.

"When you moved us up here, I never thought I would be living like a fucking peasant." Tamia's mom, Mariana Santiago, screamed out to Tamia's father in her thick Spanish accent. "You said you gave all of this drug dealer shit up back home, and it's obvious that you never did.

I just had our second baby, and she doesn't even recognize who you are when you come around. You spend every minute of every day on these rat-infested streets and leave us here to care for ourselves. I'm sick and tired of living like this, and if you can't give us the life you promised us, then I want to go back home, and when I leave, my kids are coming with me," Mariana declared meaning every single word.

"Tee is a newborn, and she is not going to remember these times," Delino Santiago, Tammy's father, responded in his thick island accent. "I'm just going to get the team together out here, and then I'll be more available for the family."

"Cut the shit," Mariana responded. "I heard it when I was back home in Honduras. That's why I followed you to the Cayman Islands. I was even patient and handled the household alone while you set up your team in Jamaica.

I'm almost thirty, and I never expected to be living my life like this. I'm sick of this shit!" Mariana had been silent for a long time, but she couldn't hold it in anymore.

When Mariana and Delino met, they couldn't stand each other. As a hostess on a yacht, Mariana had dealt with her share of entitled rich men. Delino Santiago, in her opinion, was the worst of them.

He was tall, attractive as hell, and charming. Because his father was a politician with deep pockets, Delino Santiago was untouchable, and he knew it. No was not a word that he was used to hearing. Well, until the day he ran into Mariana.

***

"No," Mariana declared as she stared the young man directly into his eyes. "I can say it for you in English if you would like. I should warn you; it sounds the same." Mariana continued in her native langue. "There are plenty of other women on this boat to play around with. Go try one of them." Without allowing him the opportunity to rebuttal, Mariana walked away.

For months, Mariana kept her interactions with Delino as short as they needed to be. Whenever he attended an event, she always did her best to be as busy as possible. She did all of that because she never wanted him to know that underneath that tough exterior, a woman had grown fond of their odd connection.

"Good evening," Delino whispered in Mariana's ear. She had been so busy preparing a drink for one of the guests that she didn't notice when he snuck behind her. "I got you something," he continued as he pulled out a small silver box and handed it to her. "Open it."

"Sorry," Mariana started as she stepped back. "I don't accept gifts from strangers. Why don't you try giving it to another woman on here? I'm sure someone else will gladly take whatever it is."

Delino knew she would give him a hard time, but he hoped she would have opened the damn box first. "Look, I overheard you and one of your girls talking about how unsafe your living situation is," he started as he leaned in closer to her. "I just happened to have one of my houses open up. I want you to take it."

Mariana stood there, scanning his eyes. She wanted to know why he wouldn't just leave her alone. Growing up, Mariana had always been protected since she was the youngest of seven kids. Everyone knew not to mess with her because her brothers loved making an example of anyone who tried. That was all before her older siblings ventured in different directions as they all aspired for a better life for themselves. For the first time, Mariana was stuck in a cold world, fending for herself in every way possible.

Sure, his offer sounded great, but she was no fool. Eventually, there would be a cost to pay - and she damn sure couldn't afford it.

"It's rude to eavesdrop," Mariana said as she stepped back again. "Anyway, while I am grateful for the offer, I'm going to have to decline." Mariana turned to walk away, but for the first time since they had met, Delino was determined, like never before, to have a different encounter with her.

Without much force, he grabbed her arm to turn her back in his direction. Even though she would never admit it, Mariana had fantasized about this moment several times. She always wondered if there was any bite behind all of his barking. Apparently, there was.

"You're going to accept my gift," Delino said softly as he leaned in closer. "Because you deserve it and more. If you want to accept it as a tenant and pay rent, I'm cool with that. If you want to be my woman, you have that option too." He put his other hand behind her back and pulled her in closer. "Which option is it going to be?"

Mariana didn't know how to respond. On one hand, her body had never felt the intense passion that was coursing through her. Most men were too intimidated by her mouth to do what Delino just did. On the other hand, she refused to be just another notch on his belt.

"Well," she started softly. "I think..." was all she could muster before Delino began chuckling.

"Why can't you just admit that you're in love with me," he asked her boldly. "This relationship would work so much better if you did."

"Oh, please," Mariana snapped back as she pulled away from his embrace. "You must be confusing me for someone else."

"That's impossible," Delino spat back confidently. "No one in this world gives me a headache like you."

Mariana laughed at his response, and Delino used that as an opportunity to pull her back into his embrace. This time, Mariana welcomed the embrace by stepping in closer.

For a moment, she allowed herself to imagine what it would be like if she allowed herself to be honest about her feelings for him. *Would he always be this charming?* She wondered. After not having an example of a healthy, loving relationship, Mariana decided that love and marriage was not for her. *Will I regret not taking him up on his offer?*

***

Delino Santiago was a businessman, but before he was anything, he was also a smart man.

As much as he wanted to put his family in a comfortable home, like the villas they just moved from, he knew it would bring too much heat his way, and he wanted to stay off of the radar. Although he had his family living in one of the roughest spots in Dorchester, Massachusetts, he always made sure that they were well protected.

"Give me a year, and I promise you that things won't be like this," Lino promised, softening his tone and pulling Mariana in to embrace her.

Mariana stepped back from him. "I've given you the best years of my life Lino, and this is where I am today. You're out all hours of the night doing God knows what with only God knows who, and I'm here taking care of a family and trying to protect our newborn from these fucking roaches. I can't do this anymore, Lino, and I refuse to do it for another second." She turned to walk away.

Delino grabbed her arm and turned her back to face his direction. "You should really watch your mouth and realize who the fuck you're speaking to before I get angry," Delino whispered softly. He was doing his best not to get angry with his wife, but she always chose the worst moments to vent about her fucking feelings.

"I'm not doing shit," she spat back with venom in her voice and fire in her eyes.

"You ungrateful bitch," Delino roared. The thunderous sound of his voice caused the young infant to wake up screaming.

Instead of immediately going to tend to her daughter like she normally would have, the sight of a bug on the wall, his words, and the fact that he woke the baby up Mariana into a rage.

"Get angry then motherfucker because I have had enough of you and all of your shit! You think cause you pay a few raggedy bills that you have the right to talk to me any way you want to? It's about time that I let you know that those days will be over if you don't learn to fucking respect-," before she was able to finish her statement, Delino slapped her with all of his might.

Mariana's small 5'1" frame was no match for Lino, who was 6'3 and 250 pounds of pure muscle.

"Shut up, bitch," he yelled out. "Let me explain something to you. I can do what the fuck I want because I am the man of this house. Regardless of how raggedy this place is do you have any idea how many other bitches would *kill* to be in the position that you're in," he asked as he stood over the frail young woman. "I'm going to give you two options, and you better choose wisely.

Being the generous man that I am, I will let you leave here with the clothes on your back, if that is what you choose. Otherwise, you can pack a bag, and I'll take you back home for a week's vacation, and we can act like this never happened. You have until I make it home from this run to have your answer.

You just better make sure that my children don't leave this house until I get back, or no matter what you choose, you will regret not listening to my orders." Delino demanded before he slammed the door shut to their tiny apartment.

As much as Mariana wanted to pack her bags and leave with her children, she knew it wouldn't be wise to do it. Delino had a lot of pull no matter where he was, and she knew that no matter what, she always had eyes on her.

She always loved the added security because she knew that what Delino did was dangerous. Still, it was times like this that made her feel like a prisoner in her own home.

With no other options, she decided to pack her bags to head back to her home country for a vacation.

"Tamia Santiago I don't ever want you to allow a man to put you through what I have to go through just to survive." Mariana spoke to her infant child as if she could understand. "You're a queen, and you deserve to be treated and respected like one. I will make sure that you know and understand that if it's the last thing I do on this Earth."

| 3 |

Where is My Father?

"You're nothing but an ungrateful bitch! I brought you here from a third-world country and showed you what life has to offer, and this is how you re-pay me? You think you can come in here whenever you feel like and do whatever the hell you want and not have to answer to anyone." the distraught Mariana screamed out at Tammy.

"Just because you're 16 now does not mean that you're a grown woman and get to do whatever the hell you want! You have no idea how many children would wish to have the opportunities that you had, and now you're just throwing it all away."

Although Tammy hated to admit when her mother was right, she knew that she was more blessed than most by her wonderful up-bringing. Tammy and her family were the only minorities in the small gated community of Sweet Water that she lived in. At the age of 16, Tammy didn't have to work because everything she had ever wanted was handed to her. Still, Tammy didn't like depending on other people and instead would do whatever she had to in order to survive on her own.

"You always told me to go out and get things for myself, and that is exactly what I'm doing. It's so hypocritical of you to judge how I want to make my money," Tammy responded.

"Stealing is not the way. I always taught you that if something was meant for you, then it would be there for you when you had the money to buy it."

"Come on, mom. I don't steal anything for just my personal gain. I cop a few products at work and flip them to put money in my pocket, and I take care of myself so that way you can save a few extra dollas in your pocket. What's da problem?"

"You better remember who the hell you're talking to like that. I am not one of these hoodlums you run around with. You are not going to disrespect me, and you will not speak to me in slang either.

I raised you with some common sense so you can spare me with the idiotic vocabulary that you're picking up from your 'so called' friends," Mariana stated.

Tammy worked at a beauty supply store and had always been known as the Weave Queen. Although Tammy had naturally long and curly hair, she loved making new wigs and helping other girls feel better by hooking up their hair. No one could touch her make-up and hair skills, and instead of keeping the talent to herself, she decided to use it to make extra money.

During new shipments, she would only count a certain amount of the inventory that her store received. Then, she would use the rest that wasn't counted in to handle her own business.

"It doesn't matter who my friends are because I'm always going to be me. The paycheck that these people give me every two weeks is a joke, and what I'm doing is making me hundreds of dollas a day. How many adults do you know capable of making the kind of money that I'm making? I'm going to live the life I'm supposed to, and I'm prepared to get it any way necessary."

"So I guess that's why you're skipping school now too, then huh," Mariana asked. "You don't think I haven't talked to your teachers who tell me that they are surprised when they finally get an opportunity to see your face in class? Almost all of your teachers agreed that because you're so intelligent, neither one of them wants to fail you, but they will have to if you continue to not appear in class."

"Those teachers want to tell me how to live my life, but look what they're doing. They work mad hours a week for a room full of unappreciative children and get a lousy paycheck. I really don't see the point in wasting my time with school if that is what the outcome of their hard work equates out to," Tammy spat back.

"I'm doing what I love. I can spend money like crazy because it's coming in faster than I can spend it. Why are you not happy that one of your kids is self-sufficient at a young age instead of trying to depend on you and ya man to take care of things for me," Tammy asked - seriously confused.

"It's sickening to me that out of you and your brother, you were the one to spend the least amount of time with your father, but you act the most like him.

I moved you away from him and that lifestyle because I wanted more for you. I've told you many times about your father's profession, and you have seen firsthand how that impacts some of the people hooked on the products that he sells. You're doing something like this, but it's only a matter of time before this money becomes little to you, and you'll become greedy and want to find more ways to make it."

"Ma, I've told you before, and I'll tell you again. I don't agree with my father's lifestyle, and that is why he and I don't deal with each other now. The man comes in and out of my life whenever he feels like it because his job seems to be more important than his family. I would never want to deal with him deeper because I know he'll always choose that over me, and I'll never be that way myself," she declared with much confidence. "No matter what, my priorities are all together."

"I get it. You're young and dumb and think you know it all, but I can't let your stubbornness put me into an early grave when I still have three other children to raise. I considered sending you to boot camp, but I know that is going to do nothing at all. You're a smooth talker and will somehow manage to talk your way outta something that is supposed to benefit you, so I'm sending you to stay with your father for the summer. Maybe if you get a chance at what it is really like to be around him, you will understand why I am the way that I am with you."

Tammy and Mariana had always had a tumultuous relationship. Tammy was Mariana's oldest daughter, and out of all of her children, she was the most like her. Neither one of them wanted to be wrong or outspoken by the other one, and they were both stubborn enough to fight as long as they needed to in order to prove a point.

"You seem to forget that no matter what, I am the adult, and you are the child. I will no longer tolerate your blatant disrespect for what I am trying to raise you to be," Mariana declared.

Tammy was surprised that her mother would stoop to such a level because Tammy had always made it known that she had no desire to develop a relationship with her father.

"That man is dead to me, and you know it! Why the hell would you ever think that it's a good idea to send me to stay with him - even if it's only for a few months? Oh, I get it," she snickered. "I'm younger than you, and I've made more money this year than you've made in your entire life, so now you're jealous," Tammy said with a slight evil chuckle. "You want to tell me about life when you're laying up in here waiting for the next nigga to take care of you instead of going out and getting your own. When you can –," before Tammy could finish her sentence, she felt the power of her mother's right fist to her jaw.

"You think that just because you're too old to get your ass whooped with a belt that you're a woman now? Well, since you want to play woman, then I'm going to treat you and handle you like one. I refuse to let a bitch talk to me any kind of way, and I damn sure won't tolerate this shit in my own house," she snarled. "You should consider yourself lucky that I don't ship you off to live with him permanently. I need a vacation from you and your antics for a little while. You're leaving tomorrow. Pack your bags. Your brother is going to take you to the airport in the morning. Ciao," Mariana said as she stormed out of the room, leaving Tammy there alone with her anger and frustration.

***

Tammy had never been to New York. On different circumstances, she would have been ecstatic to be spending her summer in the state that was known for its excitement and fashion. She was not prepared to spend so much time with her father. Tammy hardly had many memories of her father, but the ones she did have of him were not pleasant. She had been within earshot and heard several nasty and hurtful conversations between her mother and her father and blamed him for her parents' issues.

When Tammy was only 5 years old, her mother had remarried to her stepfather, Richard, and everything she knew had changed. Her mother had more children and moved Tammy and her siblings away from all of their friends and family in Boston to follow Richard's job in Florida.

Richard tried his hardest to build a healthy relationship with Tammy. Still, Tammy was not interested, and she made it clear. Because of the anger and animosity that she had felt about her mother's decision to remarry and move to a state she hated, she often would rebel just to piss them off. She would often break curfew, talk back, steal, and get in trouble at school.

Usually, when Mariana was pissed off with Tammy, she would threaten her with the idea of either boot camp or moving to live with her father. Tammy never thought her mother would actually have the heart to do it.

"This is all my fault," Mariana said as she stood over Tammy while she finished packing the last of her belongings. "I cared too much to give you the things I never had growing up, and now it seems that you feel you are entitled to the life you've been given. It's about time that you get the wake-up call that you deserve."

Her mother didn't show her any affection or kind words before she slammed the door shut once Tammy had all of her bags on the front doorstep.

Her flight was only two and half hours, but it seemed much longer than that to Tammy. All she could think about the entire time was the money she was losing every minute she wasn't available for her clients. When the plane landed and she reached her destination, she exited the plane's doors and went down to the baggage claim to retrieve her stuff.

Once she had secured all of her belongings, she began to look around for her father.

"This is crazy," she thought to herself. *"I don't even know what the motherfucker I'm looking for really even looks like in person now."*

After searching the crowd for what seemed like forever, she finally noticed three girls standing next to a sign that read "Welcome Home Tee." She walked over in their direction with hopes that she could find her ride home.

"Welcome home, Tee," the girls said with much excitement when Tammy got closer to them.

Tammy was normally very social and outgoing, but she found it hard to be as welcoming to these strangers as they were to her due to her current circumstance.

"Where is my father," Tammy asked coldly. "Also, Tee is a name reserved for close family and friends. Ya'll can call me Tammy."

"He's at home waiting for you," the short, petite one responded. "I'm Tanya," she declared cheerfully with a smile a mile long. "These are my sister. That's my older sister Nina," she said as she pointed to the tall, miserable-looking one. "That's our baby sister Tiffany," she said, pointing to the very large and round one. "Your dad asked us to come get you to hopefully give you some time to get used to being in the big city."

"That's great," Tammy huffed. "He hasn't seen me almost all my life, and he didn't even have the decency to pick me up on his own. I'm sure this is going to be an interesting trip."

"Shit," the round one spoke up. "I wish my daddy was yo' daddy. I wouldn't complain if I was you."

"That's easy to say," Tammy responded without bothering to look in her direction. "He isn't your dad, so you don't know what kind of father he actually is. Can we please just hurry up and get out of here? I've had a long day, and I just want to get where I gotta go."

None of the girls responded as they could clearly tell that Tammy was annoyed and not in the mood for socializing. They all immediately gave into her request to cut the meeting short to head home without saying another word.

Tammy had only been in New York for a short while and was already experiencing a huge culture shock. Growing up in an affluent area of Orlando, Florida, Tammy's version of projects and hoods was much different than that of what she saw. People were friendlier, and it was not uncommon to strike up a conversation with a total stranger. However, people up north just seemed to be too busy and self-indulged in their own lives and problems to even offer a smile to someone walking by who might need it.

"Your dad owns a few spots out here, but for some reason, he chooses to live over here in Bedford-Stuyvesant," Nina said as she parked the car. "Nobody calls it that out here, though. We all just call it Bed-Stuy.

Your dad lives in this building on the third floor. Go put your shit up, and we'll show you around."

"I'll come up with you," Tanya said. "You're new here, and I don't want nobody thinking they can fuck wit you."

Tammy didn't want to be impolite, but she wondered what kind of protection Tanya's small ass would be able to offer her when she was not even five feet and maybe 100 pounds dripping wet. Instead of saying what she really wanted to reply, she just shook her head, grabbed her shit, and got out of the car.

The moment she opened the door, she was greeted with loud sounds of music blasting from a few of her father's neighbors. She glanced over at the place that would be her home for the next few months. She noticed all of the different flags hanging out from the windows and all of the kids playing in the middle of the street. She even saw some old lady talking to herself and shaking her keys over her head as she walked down the block.

"Your pops says you from Florida," Tanya started. "I bet this is mad different from home."

"You have no idea," Tammy responded.

"Brooklyn isn't as bad as it looks or appears on the movies and T.V. It just takes some getting used to, is all," Tanya continued. "Watch your stuff, don't stare at nobody. Oh, and if shit pops off, you didn't see or hear nothing."

Before they made it up the stairs to the large building that her father lived in, a couple of boys called out at them from the bottom of the stairs. "Ayo shorty," one boy screamed out. "Come here, let me talk to you."

Tanya turned around to see who was talking to them.

"Damn. That's Derrick," Tanya whispered. "He's fine, has money, and I heard his pipe game was crazy. You need to go talk to that one."

Tammy didn't take Tanya's advice and instead continued walking up the stairs to put her bags down.

She entered the building without a code or being buzzed in as one of the neighbors was leaving the same time she was going in. Her father lived in a three-story family home, so she just went up to the third floor and knocked on the door.

Tammy had seen pictures of her father, and her mother had told her several times of the large stature of her father's frame. Still, she was surprised to see it for herself in person when he opened the door. Despite seeing him earlier on in her life, everything about her father was a vague memory.

"Hey Tee," he said as he grabbed her bags and suitcases that she had been carrying.

"What up," she responded.

She followed him into his house and took a look around. She immediately noticed that her father wasn't much of a decorator, and no one would be able to tell from the place that he called home that he was supposed to be loaded.

"Through that door over there is your room," Delino started. "Make yourself at home. If you need anything, just let me know."

"Well, I'm about to go with these girls to check out the city," Tammy responded. "I need a key and the code to get in when I get back."

"No," he responded. "I always leave someone in my home when I leave, so you don't have to worry about not having a way in."

Tammy thought it was weird that her father didn't want her to have her own set of keys but didn't want to press the issue too much.

"Ok," she replied awkwardly. "I guess I'll be going now."

"It's different seeing you in person compared to your pictures."

"You too," she responded before leaving and closing the door behind her.

When Tammy made it back outside, she noticed Tanya flirting with one of Derrick's friends. Instead of joining Tanya, Derrick, and his two friends, she just walked over to the car that Nina and Tiffany were still sitting in.

"Didn't you hear me call you," Derrick asked with an attitude as Tammy passed him.

"I'm sorry," she said, matching his demeanor. "I didn't realize you were speaking to me, seeing as how Ayo or shorty are nowhere on my birth certificate."

"You got a smart ass mouth," he responded.

"And you clearly don't have any class and don't know how to deal with a lady." Tammy placed her hand on her hip. "Is this what the hell you were calling me over here for? If so, I got other shit to do right now; I can play games with you later."

"I was going to tell you that I thought you were sexy," Derrick responded. "I was thinking about getting to know you, but never mind now."

"Oh, how will I ever recover," she asked sarcastically. Without another word, she left Derrick standing there to bask in his first real rejection.

Tiffany and Nina got out of the car once Tammy finally made it back to where they were. Without waiting for their sister, the girls decided to just walk around and show Tammy the rest of the neighborhood.

"What was you and Derrick talking about," Nina asked immediately.

"Not a damn thing. He tried to rap, and I wasn't hearing it," Tammy responded. "I've heard for the longest about some New York pizza, and I'm hungry as shit. Let's go get some."

"How," Tiffany asked. "We don't got no damn money."

"Ya'll don't have a couple dollas to grab some food with? What the fuck ya'll be doing out here?"

"Not all of us come from the same shit you do," Tiffany said with an attitude.

"Let's clear something up right here and now. Nobody takes care of me. I live with my peoples because I'm not old enough to go out and get my own shit yet.

Whatever dead presidents you see me with is because I fucking earned them my damn self. I'll buy y'alls a slice. Just take me where I can get the best pizza. Also, don't ever let a nigga make you do his work for him for free," Tammy continued. "My father should have paid ya'll for taking care of his business today. Knowing him, it's probably too late to ask for anything because the job is done. But next time, get in the habit of asking for your shit upfront."

They were halfway down the block when Tammy noticed another group of boys trying to get their attention from across the street.

"Damn, bitch! That's Jarrod and Jeremy. Let's go talk to them," Nina suggested.

"Ya'll can go. I'll be right over here," Tammy said.

Without another word, she watched the two sisters practically run across the street to see what the young men wanted.

Tammy looked around and noticed the old woman who had been talking to herself sitting in front of the stoop staring at her. Once she made eye contact with the woman, she signaled for Tammy to come closer.

Tammy was naturally curious and had to go over there to see what the old woman wanted.

"Who the hell are you? I have never seen you over here before," the old woman asked.

"I'm Tammy," she responded. "I'm just here visiting my father."

The women's eyes grew wide, and her bottom lip dropped in amazement. She got up from the chair she was sitting in and hugged Tammy, who stood there awkwardly waiting for the woman to get off her.

"Dios Mio," she said in Spanish. "I haven't seen you since you were a little baby. Your mother, Mariana, and I used to be friends. We worked together on a yacht back home in Honduras as service attendants to rich men." The woman caught on to the clearly confused look on Tammy's face and thought it would be best to elaborate.

"My name is Estrella Cruz, and get your mind out of the gutter," she chuckled. "Rich men just seem to prefer beautiful women in bikinis making their food, drinks, and catering to their every request. Now don't get me wrong, some women fell prey to the money, drugs, and fast life and thought getting paid for sexual activities would get them a chance to be with some wealthy men. Instead, they just passed them around until they got tired of them. I think that's why your father, Lino, fell for your mother and why my sweet Lorenzo fell for me."

Just as it seemed like the woman was going to get deep into an interesting story, Tiffany and Nina walked up.

"Stop telling that girl those lies, you crazy ass old lady," Tiffany yelled out angrily.

"You always telling that same fucking story, but my mama said that shit can't be true because you've been lonely and crazy as long as she's known you." Tanya, who finally managed to stop flirting long enough to join Tammy and her sister's, joined in on the taunting.

In the time that Tammy had been talking to the woman, she had heard a pronounced Spanish accent, but once the girls came up, her English became very hard to understand. "Fuck you and your mother," Ms. Cruz responded in a thick accent.

"Ir con tus amigo," she then told Tammy with a snare.

Tammy wanted to hear the rest of the story but didn't want to further aggravate her. Without saying another word, she did as she was told and turned to leave with them.

"Por ahora, vamos mantener este encuentro entre nosotros," Ms. Cruz screamed out after they had walked off a good distance.

The fact that she wanted to keep their meeting and conversation a secret just made Tammy even more curious about the strange woman she had just met.

| 4 |

Treat Your Temple Like it's Worth More Than Gold

"Are you still a young lady," Delino asked Tammy over the meal she had prepared for them.

"What do you mean by that," Tammy responded.

"Have you had sex," he asked, not making eye contact with her to make the conversation any weirder than it already was.

"You realize that I'm 16 years old right," she asked him with pure attitude dripping from her tone. "You're a little too late to be playing the concerned daddy role, don't you think?"

"I've been really patient with you, but this attitude of yours is getting real old - fast," Delino responded as he placed his fork down and moved his napkin from his lap to the table. "I'm your father, and you will respect me. You've been here for a little over a week now, and you never speak to me." Delino paused for a moment as he pushed some food around his plate. "When you do open your mouth, it's only to say something smart as hell, and I'm already sick of this shit."

Tammy could sense a little sincerity in his tone to get to know his only daughter. Still, she couldn't look past the years of disappointment and heartbreak that his lack of effort had left her with. "You've been absent almost my whole fucking life! What did you expect this was going to be like, huh? Did you expect me to jump for joy that you are actually pretending to be a daddy for the first time in your life? Did you expect that I would sit up in the house playing with dolls with cute little barrettes in my hair, huh? What the hell could you have fucking expected for a child you rejected and neglected." Tammy spat each word on more harshly than the one before it. "Anyway, I'm already having sex, so you can save your birds and bees conversations for some other child that you're probably not taking care of," she fired back.

"That's your damn problem," Delino said as he stood up from the table. "You think you're grown and that no one can teach you shit about you or life. All I know is I don't want you bringing any pissed-tailed boys or fucking babies in my damn house.

Respect your body. No man will ever respect another man's whore. Diamonds, pearls, and gold are hard to get, and only a worker that works hard enough gets the pleasure of finding one. Treat your temple like it's worth more than gold." Delino pushed his chair in and walked out of the dining room, leaving Tammy alone with just her anger and her thoughts.

***

"Your father loves you very much," Ms. Cruz tried to assuage Tammy after she got through explaining her most recent quarrel with her father.

Since their first conversation, Tammy had been looking for an excuse to come talk to the neighborhood crazy lady. The recent exchange of frustration with her father was the opportunity she had been waiting for.

"Well, he has a peculiar way of showing it. The man has been absent my entire life, and for some strange reason, he thinks he can try to play Daddy of the year. He forgets I'm no longer a little girl anymore. He decided to worry about these streets more than me when I needed him. Anyway, his fake attempts at parenthood are a little too late. I'm damn near a woman already."

"Girl, please. You hardly have enough hair on your pussy, and you think you're grown," Ms. Cruz said while holding back a laugh. "The moment you think you have all of the answers to life's problems is the moment you've set yourself up to fail. Make it a point to learn something new every day and make sure to listen also. You might never use the advice that the other person gives, but you never know what you can learn from someone walking in a different path than you."

"So then tell me, why do you pretend to be crazy when everyone else is around," Tammy asked bluntly.

"I should have known that your nosey ass would ask that eventually. Bring your ass in the house," she said as she stood up from her place on the stoop.

Tammy followed her into the apartment building, and they both were in complete silence. She followed her up three flights of stairs before they finally reached their destination. Tammy watched her fumble through what looked like hundreds of keys before she finally found the one she was searching for.

"Life is all about perception. How I see something will be different than how you view the same thing. I don't care what people think about me. Because at the end of the day, I know the truth. I prefer for people to think I'm crazy for two reasons. One, the moment I get tired of the disrespect and retaliate, they have no idea what hit them. Two, how many people do you know that want to mess with a crazy person," she chuckled. "They don't try to rob me or mess with me because they don't know what I'm fully capable of. Normally people leave me alone, but your bum-ass friends still haven't learned just yet."

"Those broads are not my friends. They are just the only girls I've met since I've been up here. I usually don't even cool it with females like that, but I haven't had any issues with them."

"Yet," Ms. Cruz corrected her. "Those bitches are the only friends they got. That's usually a dead giveaway. They hardly travel out of Brooklyn, but no other females deal with them like that. Doesn't that seem a little bit strange to you?"

"I guess so. As long as they don't cross me, then they are good," Tammy responded.

"You'll learn, and since you don't want to listen to me, you'll just have to feel. Anyway, it's best to be by your damn self than to just have a couple of phony cronies smiling all in your damn face. You know birds of a feather flock together. You either fly with pigeons and vultures or soar with eagles. You can't do both. You don't want the reputation of those around you to speak to others before you get a chance to."

"Yeah, I hear you, Ms. Cruz," Tammy responded.

"I'm sure you do, but you need to stop just hearing and actually listen, damn it."

"Tell me about Lorenzo," Tammy asked, trying to change the direction of the conversation.

"I thought you would have been more interested in finding out about your parents or the reason that I asked you to keep our meeting last week a secret," Ms. Cruz responded.

"I am, but it was something in the way your demeanor changed when you talked about him that makes me curious to know more.

I love to read or listen to a really entertaining story," Tammy stated.

"I could sit here for hours, days, and weeks talking about my sweet Lorenzo, but on days like today, I just don't feel like going back to that part of my life. The time I spent with that man was truly my happiest and most memorable time on this Earth. Days like today just make me wish it never had to end." Her tough demeanor briefly faded as she began talking so highly about the man she was clearly still passionately in love with.

"Anyway, you're too young to fully understand our story. I'll share it in more detail when I feel you're really ready to truly listen and appreciate the story."

"So then why did you ask me to keep our meeting a secret," Tammy asked another question to again change the mood of the conversation.

"I asked you to keep it a secret because I really wanted you to hear my side of the story before you heard anything from tus padres.

Your mom was my best friend decades ago, and I loved that woman like my own sister at one point. Still, sometimes people don't always trust your intentions because of fear of getting hurt again.

Delino is a well-respected man back home, and anywhere that he was, he was about making money and running his business," she said with a wink.

"I already know. He sold stuff that kills people every day. He forgot about his family all for the high of chasing money," Tammy stated.

"Did your father ever tell you that personally," Ms. Cruz questioned Tammy.

"Well, no. Not exactly, but..." is all Tammy could say before she was cut off.

"But you don't know a damn thing," she responded flatly. "You came down here knowing half of the story and already had an opinion formed on the kind of man that you think he is. How do you ever expect to learn shit with a closed mind and heart? Even if your dad wanted to explain himself to you, you aren't leaving him with an open door that he could feel comfortable walking through.

You know, the Lord doesn't bless us with the same visions. We don't all love the same or feel the same pain. Hell, no two humans ever walk the same path, so never judge anyone based off of what they do or why they do whatever it is that they do. You either learn to love them, or you don't fuck with them. It's that easy. At the end of this entire journey, there is only one person whose judgment truly matters. That's why it is important to never lose sleep over the opinions of others or stress yourself out worrying about what the next person is doing." Ms. Cruz got up from the spot on the couch that she had been sitting in.

"I don't know how I managed to bring you up in my home, allow you to get comfortable, and give you so much knowledge for free. Get your ass off my couch, and let's go back outside," she demanded.

Usually, Tammy didn't like taking orders from anyone. Hell, she wasn't even used to taking them from her mother without saying something slick. Still, she had a strong feeling that it wouldn't be a good idea to respond to Ms. Cruz how she really wanted to. Instead, she got up and did as she was told without a single complaint.

They both went back outside and went back to their previous positions on the stoop in front of Ms. Cruz's building. Just as Tammy sat down, she noticed Derrick and two of his friends walking down the block on the other side of the street.

Tammy had to give it to him; he was always well dressed and definitely good-looking. It was easy to tell why Tanya and so many other girls in the neighborhood seemed to just go crazy over him. He stood 5'11, and his dark black complexion was free of blemishes or scars. All of his teeth were straight and white; add to that the two-deep dimples, and it made his beautiful smile almost hypnotizing.

"Ay," he began to yell in Tammy's direction. Instead of finishing what he was going to initially say, he simply smiled and decided to approach her differently.

"Tammy," he yelled to her. "Come here."

"Are you two legs broken," she yelled back sarcastically. "You come here."

Derrick wasn't used to working so hard to get a female to talk to him, but he figured he would play along with her.

Tammy excused herself from her spot on the stoop and walked to the edge of the sidewalk to see what he wanted.

"What up shorty," he asked when he made it to where she was standing.

"I thought we had a pretty clear understanding the last time that we spoke that you would only address me by name. How did you know my name anyway," she asked.

"Ya girl had to tell me since you was acting so stuck up the last time we spoke," he replied with a chuckle.

"As a matter of fact," she started. "I wasn't acting stuck up. I just had to make sure that you knew that the half-ass compliments and that little bit of attention you were trying to show me only works for those birds you're used to dealing with. I'm not them and wanted to make sure you knew that. Obviously, it worked because you actually approached me like you had some sense today," she joked.

"Yeah, aight," he replied. "I guess you right. Check this out, though; I'm trying to take you out. What you doing later tonight?"

"I'll be busy. I'm still trying to get settled in," Tammy responded flatly.

"So then when are you going to be free," Derrick questioned.

"I guess whenever I feel like I'm all settled in."

"Give me your number, and I'll call you, and we'll set something up," Derrick persisted.

"Or, you can give me your number, and when I'm free, I'll call you," Tammy responded.

"You're really stubborn," he declared.

"You don't know the half of it."

Tammy took out her Nokia 3310 and handed it to him so he could save his number in it.

"I saved my house, cell, and pager number, so don't give me no shit about why you don't hit me up," Derrick said before he walked away to join his boys that were impatiently waiting on him.

"I guess you're not like those hoes you hang out with after all," Ms. Cruz stated as Tammy took her seat next to her.

"I thought you're not supposed to judge anyone. Isn't that what you said," Tammy asked.

"I'm not. I'm just calling them exactly what they are. Those girls would have jumped at the opportunity you just had with that boy."

"Well I'm not like that," she said flatly. "I may not always listen to my mother, but the stuff I do follow is always the important stuff."

"In my experience, girls who grow up without their daddies around always end up being the hoes," Ms. Cruz stated.

"I can see how that could be true," Tammy replied. "It used to bother me not having my dad around, and sometimes I wanted that male attention that I wasn't getting from him. I was eleven the last time I let my dad in just for him to walk out again. I made the decision then and there that he was dead. It was easier to think that he was done and gone than to realize that the man is still living and just doesn't care enough about me to make a relationship work.

I have my two brothers, my step pops, and my homeboys back home. That's all the male attention that I really need."

"Homeboys," Ms. Cruz started. "Is that what you are now calling the men you sleep with?"

"Hell no," she retorted. "We play ball, video games, and just relax. I'm just like one of the guys back home. Well, I was anyway. I started working at this beauty supply store almost a year ago and got into make-up and dressing a little more girly. Now, those idiots have started thinking with their little heads instead of remembering I'm the same Tammy I've always been. I just wear clothes that flatter my body and make-up now."

"Sweetie, take this from an old lady who has lived what feels like a million lives. Most men do more thinking with their little head than their big one. Some idiots can't even think straight in the presence of a beautiful woman. Those damn fools," she chuckled. "If you continue to play that one like you are, you could have him eating out of the palm of your hands without ever having to touch him."

"Oh for real? What would make you say that about him," Tammy asked.

"A guy like him has too much pride to accept rejection. He's not going to give up until he feels satisfied that he's conquered you. Lorenzo taught me that."

"How," Tammy asked, hoping she would have already forgotten about her previous decision not to talk about him.

"Dios mio," Ms. Cruz exclaimed. "You ask a lot of damn questions. You really should be a reporter or something."

"My mom says that to me all the time," Tammy laughed. "I love to read, write, and ask a lot of questions, so maybe that would be a good field for me. I'm just a naturally curious person, and the only stupid questions are the ones you don't ask, right?"

"Yeah, yeah, whatever. Luckily for you, I like you, and I don't mind answering your questions, but not everyone else is going to feel the same way. After a while, I start to feel like I'm being interrogated and that you might be working for the other side. You better learn how to make people give up the information you need voluntarily instead of making them feel like what they say could incriminate them.

Anyway, I met Lorenzo on that yacht I was telling you about. He was a pilot and had flown in to visit because your father had explained to him just how beautiful Honduras was.

His first night in town and on that yacht was a night that I worked. He was 6'5" and had pecan-tanned skin. His blue eyes and physique made him impossible to miss even in a crowded room.

Everything about him told me he was Spanish, but just from a different country. Pero he looked just like un gringo," she said as a little smile crept on her face. "When he would speak, everyone stopped and paid attention. He seemed like he was the King and the words he spoke were like gold to everyone who was within his presence. That confidence and charisma just oozed off of him, and even with our language barrier, I knew he was smart as hell.

Lorenzo was Brazilian and spoke Portuguese and English, and at the time, I only knew Spanish. I was no fool and knew that he found me and the fact that I didn't chase after him like most women very attractive. I knew he would sleep with me the moment I allowed him to, but I didn't have sex with him immediately. Hell, I didn't even have sex with him for the first year we were together. He respected me, and it was because I gave him something to appreciate. Women were constantly throwing themselves at him, but he wanted the one he felt like he couldn't have.

All I'm trying to say is treat yourself and your body like it's priceless. You can't expect anyone to value your worth if you won't do it yourself first.

I know that wasn't part of the original question you asked, but that gem was for free."

Tammy was silent for a few moments as she took a minute to absorb what Ms. Cruz just shared. "That's crazy. You waited a whole year to have sex with a man you wanted? That seems so unreal these days."

"I know, and the craziest part about it is that these broads get mad when a man calls them anything but the name their mama gave them. If you act like a hoe, dress like a hoe, and associate yourself with hoes, then what the hell else do you think a man is going to treat you like?"

"Don't say you," Tammy said defensively. "I've been with one man, and he was my boyfriend for a year before we slept together."

"Fool, you better watch your tone and remember who you're talking to. I'm not one of your friends. I know Mariana taught you some manners and that you needed to respect your elders," Ms. Cruz snapped back. "Obviously, I wasn't directing my statement specifically towards you. But it doesn't help your case that you're running around here with those dusty broads," Ms. Cruz said as she nodded her head in the direction the three sisters were in. "A hard head makes a soft ass. If you keep hanging out with those broads, then you're going to get exactly what you deserve," Ms. Cruz warned.

| 5 |

You'll Want to Answer That...

"I still don't get it," K.Y asked, obviously confused. "Most of what you've shown me and told me tonight leaves me with more questions than confirming anything that you're saying. I'm not sure how telling me a story about her relationship with her people is proving your point."

"I'm going to be honest with you," Josie said as she started to pour herself another drink. "It is going to get a lot more confusing before it actually starts to make any kind of sense. I just really need you to be patient with me and be very open-minded."

Just as she finished speaking, a call from an unknown number came through to his iPhone. He sat there, unsure if he should even answer it. Usually, all unknown calls that came to his phone were from Tammy, but she had not called him in na while. Any communication that the two of them shared was whenever she would actually answer the one number that he had for her. The only unknown calls he had received lately came from Isabella, and after their last conversation, he thought it was best to just leave her alone.

***

"You motherfuckers thought you could fuck with me and go on to live peaceful and wonderful lives," she screamed through the phone. "Fuck all of you. You all are going to find out just exactly who the fuck and I am and what the fuck I'm about," Isabella screamed out after he had finally answered her call. He had been avoiding her as she was beginning to become more erratic in the number of times she would blow down his phone.

"You lied to me. You made promises that you had no intentions of keeping – all because you wanted to be Tammy's little pet," Isabella fired out. "You used me like some fucking toy. You mind fucked me, and I'm not one to let a motherfucker get away with that. Either you're going to keep all the promises you made to me, or you're going to find out the hard way.

Don't make me show you what the fuck I'm about because trust me, you'll want to curse the day you ever met," she threatened before K.Y got sick of her rant and disconnected the call.

***

"You'll want to answer that," Josie said before she took her seat and crossed her legs. "It's very important."

"Is this really what I have to do in order to get through to you," Isabella asked as soon as K.Y answered the phone. "This could have just been a lot easier if you would have answered my last few phone calls."

"How the hell," K.Y asked as he looked at Josie to read the slight smirk she was wearing at his obvious confusion. "What the fuck kind of games are you two playing with me?"

Isabella fell into an evil chuckle that actually brought goosebumps to K.Y.'s skin.

"What do you want to know," Isabella asked once the laughter subsided. "Would you like for me to answer how I know a woman that Tammy introduced you to? Why is it that you're just now curious enough to start asking questions? I can easily think of a few questions that you should have had the balls to ask for a while now. For starters, why did you never ask Tammy why or how my vehicle was parked in front of the hotel after the night we robbed your friend? Why didn't you ever question her on just exactly who she allowed in your house from PTJ Security Systems? Why did you never question why she disappeared whenever your money or product was stolen? Why did you never question her just how much money, guns, and product you lost after you stole all of that shit from Ra? Why wouldn't you question why a woman who treats her pussy like it's golden would let a man come in and 'shag the hell out of her in your face," Isabella asked in her best attempt at a British accent.

"How the hell do you know that," K.Y asked. Only he knew that painful memory of watching the woman he loved in that position. Although he originally doubted the truth behind what Josie and Isabella had initially said to him, he was all ears now.

| 6 |

She's Envious of You...

"Damn girl, you forgot how to use a phone," Ms. Cruz asked as Tammy strolled up the stoop to greet her. "You go back home, and you forget this old lady even exists."

"Cut it out, ma," Tammy said as she leaned in to hug her and kiss her cheek. "Things were just really hectic back home. My mom didn't really take it too well that I didn't want to live with her anymore. I guess she felt some type of way because I would rather be up here with you and my dad now."

Tammy took her seat next to Ms. Cruz so they could enjoy each other's company. Sometimes they talked and laughed for hours. Other times they would sit silently, watching people maneuver through their Brooklyn block.

Thanks to all of the stoop lessons that Ms. Cruz had given Tammy about her dad, she decided to use it and actually give her father a *real* chance. The more she let her guard down, the closer they became.

After the first summer she spent with her father, she would keep in contact with him during the school year and would visit him whenever she could. After several years of going back and forth, Tammy was finally ready to settle down and start her life in New York forever.

"I knew your mother would have a problem with you having a relationship with me," Ms. Cruz started. "She seemed to forget that

I was Lorenzo's teammate. We did everything together, so of course, that means I would spend more time with her husband than she would have. No matter how many times I tried to tell her, she never seemed to understand that I didn't want Lino," Ms. Cruz stopped and let out a deep sigh.

Usually, whenever Ms. Cruz talked about her friendship with Mariana, she always kept it light and fun. She loved reminiscing about their old inside jokes, but today her trip down memory lane had a different tone.

"I did what I needed to do for myself and my man," Ms. Cruz continued. "If I'm honest, I can understand why she was so reserved. Between you and me, your dad didn't mind fucking some of her friends. So I guess that's why she felt she couldn't trust me to be any different than the rest of the girls she knew. Oh well," she said before another brief pause. "What about the little fiancé you had back home? How did he handle your decision to move," Ms. Cruz asked eagerly to find out what went wrong.

"Ugh," Tammy growled in complete disgust. "I don't know what I was thinking even accepting his ring. I guess I felt I really could live the nice quiet army wife lifestyle, but I just realized that I would be miserable living like that. Anyway, I'm only twenty years old. I have my whole life ahead of me, and after being around my mom and pops, I don't think I ever want to get married. Not to mention, my mom couldn't exactly get it right with my father either, so I'm not sure why anyone would want to waste their time with the whole marriage thing.

You know what's strange about me making that revelation is it seems like more men want to marry me now. After I gave the man his ring back, two other men I dated proposed to me in a matter of weeks. It's crazy. So many women want marriage and never get asked, and here I am constantly being asked, but I don't want it."

"Oh please," Ms. Cruz replied. "You don't know what the hell you want."

"I know I didn't want to be married to any of them and that I never want to be married. Watching my mom and Richard really does confirm that for me. I call him pops now because the older I get, the more I realize that he does actually care for me like I was one of his own kids, but I just can't fathom living my life like that. I can watch him belittle her and degrade her with a shit load of hurtful words. Once she's had enough of taking it, she'll grab a knife out of the kitchen, flatten all his tires, and then threaten to use it on him. They'll talk about how much they hate each other, and then the next thing I know we're at a party for his office executives, and they are acting like we are something straight out of the Brady Bunch.

That's exactly what I pictured my life being like when I thought of my future with my ex-fiancé. He promised that all I had to do was be there, cook, clean, and join him for his annual ball, but I knew exactly what that meant for me. He was a male whore who could not keep his penis in his pants. I can't believe I gave up dealing with my own hoes just to try to commit to an actual hoe," she huffed. "If there is anything in this world that I regret, allowing him a chance into my heart would definitely be it."

"Listen, anything that once brought you happiness and joy was not a waste or regret. He taught you whatever lesson you were supposed to learn from him."

"Yeah," Tammy responded. "That I hate cheaters, liars, and insecure men who try to control me. He had an issue with the guys that I use to keep around. You know the ones who had no hope but thought they did, so they would do whatever I wanted whenever I needed it done? He told me that I didn't need to have men around to buy or give me anything because everything I ever wanted would given to me. It's not that I just care about material things, but because it seemed like such a big deal to him, I just let them all go. I even stopped taking Derrick's calls and sending all of his gifts back to him. He said that even though he liked the fact that I was self-sufficient and knew I wasn't sleeping with them, it made him uncomfortable to know that I dealt with so many other men.

"Baby, that's just how most men are," Ms. Cruz responded. "I'm sure it doesn't help that the men in your circle would jump at any opportunity to hop between those legs of yours the moment you gave them an invitation to."

"You know how I do," Tammy replied. "After all, I learned from the best. Even after blatantly turning him down, Derrick is still buying me things and taking care of things for me, and I never even touched the man. It's been four years since I met him, I only call him or see him when it's convenient for me, yet he still hangs on to my every word like he really is in love with me or something."

"At this stage, he probably is. I don't even hear about him messing with all of these broads anymore. He probably really thinks he has a shot with you. If you wanted to be in a relationship, then why not just be with him?

"Really," Tammy asked, completely surprised that she would even ask that question. "For one, he's a drug dealer, and two, he already has way too many women chasing after him. He won't ever be able to say that he conquered this challenge, so that is out of the question."

"Why do you have such an issue with drug dealers," Ms. Cruz asked.

"Damn," Tammy exclaimed. "Am I the one now being interrogated?"

Both ladies shared a giggle. "I get it. That's how my father makes his money," Tammy began. "But I just can't agree with it. It seems like the more I try to fight it and hide from them, the more I just seem to attract them. It just doesn't make any sense to me."

"Then why don't you stop hiding and running from who you are. You know you attract what you put out and who you are. You say you want a nice man, but you complain when you meet a man that you can walk all over. It's obvious that you don't really know what you want."

"Well, I could say the same about how you were with Lorenzo. You claim to be so holier-than-thou, yet you fell head over heels for a man who killed and sold drugs."

"I see you're taking my advice of trying to get what you want without asking questions, but the student will never outsmart the master," she responded with a laugh. "I hardly ever talk about my sweet Lorenzo for you make that kind of assumption about him.

My man, like your daddy, was a gangster and not like the wanna-be thugs that you see today. These fake thugs put a couple dollars in their pocket. Yet, they don't even help put into their community or take care of the ones immediately around them. They did whatever they needed to in order to protect or provided for their families and children. Lorenzo would quickly remind me that he never committed any crime that he didn't have to do. He wasn't a killer, but if he had to be, then he would do it. He held down his kingdom, which is why I did and will always respect him for the King he was. Anyway, that's as much as you're going to get outta me. Good try, though, kid."

"I just don't get how you told Tanya and all of them the story of you and Lorenzo, but you won't tell me, and I look at you as like a grandmother to me."

"Those simple broads don't understand shit," she replied frankly. "I don't know why I even wasted my breath talking about it to those idiots. Speaking of el diablo, here comes your friend and her minions now."

"What up, Tee," Tanya asked eagerly when she and her sisters finally reached the stoop.

"Ain't shit, fam," Tammy replied. "I'm finally back for good this time, though. It feels good to actually say that I'm home now."

"Hell yeah," Tanya responded. "So why the fuck are we just sitting around her with this old ass lady?"

"Watch your fucking mouth; have some manners and respectfully speak to my grandmother."

"Hello, Ms. Cruz," Tanya said between clenched teeth with much attitude.

"Hmm," Ms. Cruz responded as she rolled her eyes. "No se sorprenda cuando llegues poco de jugar con las serpientes," she said with much attitude."

"Don't nobody speak that mira mira shit. Be a woman and say it to me in English."

Tammy immediately grabbed Tanya's arm. "I'll check for you later Ma," she said before she headed down the street to get the two of them away from each other.

"Bitch, I don't mind saying it for your simple ass to understand. I just wasn't talking to you. I *said* don't be surprised when you get bit from messing with snakes," Ms. Cruz called out.

***

"We about to party and bull shit," Tanya sang, remixing her own flavor with the lyrics to the popular Biggie song as they walked towards Tanya's house to get ready.

"I'm about to finally let you meet some of my peoples at this party tonight. You always talking about if it don't make dollas it don't make sense. But all work and no play is going to put you in an early grave, girl. You'll get to meet some of my bitches and niggas tonight, and we are going to have mad fun. Some of these hoes will be perfect clients for you, so I hope you didn't forget your business cards. You can make a lot of money rolling with me out here."

Tammy didn't feed into the hype. She never left home without her business cards. And for years, Ms. Cruz had been telling her that she has never seen Tanya or her sisters with any other friends besides each other. Tammy was looking forward to seeing just how true that was.

Just as they were reaching Tanya's building, Derrick surprised them from behind.

"Damn, Tee! You come back, and you don't even holla at your boy," Derrick asked. "It's bad enough that I never hear from you when you go home, but the least you can do is holla at me when you're going to be on one of my blocks. I only get to find shit out about you through your Myspace now. I see you're letting your online celebrity status get to your head," Derrick joked.

Tammy made a slight buzz for herself online under the name of "Ms. Bossy." It seemed like when she did live in Florida, she was not safe to go anywhere without someone from her friend's list that would recognize her and either ask for a picture or her number. She initially loved the amount of support she received because it made it easier for Tammy to meet new potential clients. But she could do without all the creepy men and their played out lines always trying to get at her.

"Cut it out," she replied with a light chuckle as she playfully punched his arm. "I'm actually trying to switch up that look now that I'm up here for good now."

"What," he exclaimed. "I know you been talking about it, but I had no idea you would have the balls to go through with it. So I'm assuming that means that you're going to make more time for ya boy and finally cut out the bullshit and hard to get shit you've been playing all of these years." Derrick declared hopefully. Ever since he first met Tammy, he knew there was something special about her. He hated the idea of anyone else getting to find out just what exactly that unique quality she possessed was.

"I'm not trying to hear all that right now," Tammy responded irritably. "Can I at least unpack and get settled in before you start coming with this bullshit?"

"Yeah, you right, ma," he said, throwing his hands up and admitting defeat. "I'll give you that this time, but hit me up soon cause I missed you."

"Yeah, yeah, whatever. You probably tell that to all of your hoes," Tammy said before she turned to walk away.

"Oh," he screamed out before they made it to Tammy's building. "I got you something and left it at your dad's house. I hope you like it."

"It's from you, so I'm sure I'll love it," Tammy said with her signature grin and a wink.

***

"Damn, bitch," Nina said once they were too far down to see Derrick anymore. "What the fuck do you do to have Derrick and the rest of these niggas acting the way they do for you," she asked.

"Don't gas her," Tanya interjected before she allowed Tammy a chance to reply. "It's not that hard, and it's nothing I couldn't show you if you were just willing to learn."

"Hoe, please," Nina replied with a laugh. "I was actually asking for you cause I was hoping you would take notes. Yeah, these niggas give you money and buy you shit, but you have to suck and fuck the whole crew for what you get. Once you do the math, you're not even making minimum wage," Nina said before they all exploded in a fit of laughter. "Tammy plays these same fools and doesn't even answer their phone calls," she managed to say when she finally got her breath.

"Whatever," Tanya huffed. "It really ain't that deep. Anyway, I like fucking and the power it gives me when I'm done messing with them," Tanya snapped back. "

"Well, actually," Tammy interjected, hoping to end the tension brewing between the two sisters. "We as women have more power until we actually sleep with them."

"Fuck that shit," Tanya replied. "I need to catch mines while putting a few dollas in my pocket. At least I'm not like you bitches that just fuck for free."

"Excuse me that I'm not some cheap prostitute that sucks for dollar menu cheeseburgers, a couple dime bags, and at most some cheap ass shoes," Tiffany said, finally speaking up.

"That's because these niggas don't want to touch you two ugly bitches with a ten-foot pole. Nina, your ass is tall and skinny, and Tiffany is short, fat, and super ugly. Maybe you bitches should worry more about why ya'll look the way you do and less about what the fuck I got going on."

No one replied to Tanya's comment, and the tension between the sisters was so thick you could cut through it with a knife. It was apparent from the change in her temperament that Tanya had enough of being the butt of her sister's jokes.

"She's envious of you," Ms. Cruz would frequently tell Tammy. "Jealousy is reasonable, but envy is not. An envious person will either want to be you, own you, or kill you. Stop hanging around your biggest threat and enemy." Ms. Cruz's advice was all Tammy could think about in that moment.

***

The party was packed just like Tanya predicted. Everyone was drinking, dancing, and having a good time.

"Yo, you are cute as hell, ma. What do I have to do to get your number," a young man whispered in Tammy's ear over the loud music.

"Well," Tammy began. "That chick you came in with is mad cute. I'd love to get a chance to style her and hook up her look for you. It would definitely be a good look for you. Don't you agree?"

"Oh yeah," he asked. "What are you some kind of hairdresser or something?"

"I do it all, papi," Tammy said in a seductive tone. "I can do hair, wigs, make-up, nails, and I'll even style her in a fly outfit for the low. Once I'm done giving your girl a complete make-over, I'll re-twist your hair for free."

Obviously, the young man took Tammy's tone, friendliness, and demeanor as someone who was interested in him. But to Tammy, it was all business.

"So that's the only way to get your number and have one-on-one time with you," he asked.

"Unfortunately," she shrugged. "I have this rule about not dealing with men that are currently involved, but depending on how this goes, we might be able to make an exception." She handed him her business card and then went back to join her friends.

"Do you know what the hell you just did," Tiffany asked with much concern. "That's Rasheeda's man, and that bitch is crazy as hell."

"I don't give a damn," Tammy replied. "If I wanted him, I could have him, and luckily for her, I don't want his ass. Ya'll know I'm all about this money. I'll get that bum to drop money, and he'll keep coming back thinking he'll have a shot. Either way, he'll win because I'll have his bitch looking good and thinking the world of him," Tammy shrugged.

The girls enjoyed the rest of their evening. Tammy took her friend's advice and stopped worrying about business for the rest of the evening.

After the DJ played the last song, the girls exited the party drunk, happy, and ready to find something else to get into. Surprisingly, they noticed Rasheeda, her man, and five of her friends waiting for them.

"So you want to fuck with my nigga," Rasheeda yelled out angrily "I'm guessing you're new around here, and your wack ass friends should have told you who the hell you were dealing with."

Not one to easily let someone else upset her, Tammy responded calmly. "You know it's really sad because I was telling your man earlier how cute I thought you were. I had absolutely no idea that you were also jealous and insecure. That shit is not cute at all," Tammy replied nonchalantly.

Rasheeda was not expecting her to have such a peaceful demeanor and calm response, so she was not sure how to respond to Tammy's comment. Not wanting to look like a punk in front of her friends, Rasheeda charged at Tammy.

"Bitch," Tanya growled fiercely as she stepped between Rasheeda and Tammy.

"If I have to tie my hair up, I am going to beat your ass," Tanya threatened, meaning every word of it. "I suggest you just turn around and leave with your peoples because you are not about to fight my girl, and I can promise you that this isn't what you want in your life."

Although Tammy wasn't much of a fighter, she had previously been in two brawls before. Whenever she did fight, she always made sure to win. In the past, her mother had threatened her about losing fights numerous times.

"I don't send you out of this house to fight," Mariana once said to Tammy. "So if you're woman enough to make trouble out in the street, you better be woman enough to fight your battles. You can trust and believe if someone else beats your ass, then you will come home to another ass whooping," Mariana meant every single word.

The only reason Tammy never backed down from a fight was because her father and step-father had always stressed to her the importance of earning and keeping respect. Even though she didn't like to, she was always down to bang whenever necessary.

Tammy had a lot of girls back in Florida that she had initially considered to be her friend, but she never had anyone offer to step up for her, much less try to fight for her like Tanya had just done.

Maybe Ms. Cruz was actually wrong about something for a change, Tammy thought to herself. *Maybe Tanya isn't so ba• after all.*

| 7 |

Tanya is Nobody's Sidekick

"You put that bitch on a high-ass pedestal," Isabella screamed through the phone. "The bitch isn't shit, never has been and never will be!

You could have had me, and we could have been happy together," she said as her tone began to soften up. "I thought we were building something in all of the time that we had been spending together. I thought we were growing closer and becoming more intimate. I wanted you more than I had ever wanted a man in my entire life. I don't understand why you just didn't want me the same way." Isabella's voice had become so soft and faint it almost sounded like she was on the brink of tears.

Kyle was tired of hearing her bitch and complain, but she clearly had information that he was desperate enough to have now.

"What the fuck does she have that I didn't," Isabella asked. "What the hell could she have given you that I wasn't practically throwing at you? Don't you realize that if you would have made the right choice that you would never have been going through this," she yelled, completely changing her tone. "Why do you have to be so hard-headed and stubborn? When will you ever learn? For crying out loud, the woman kept blowing smoke in your face the whole time, and everyone knows that where there is smoke there is always fire. How did you miss all of the minor flaws of Tammy's master plan," she asked angrily.

"That bitch Tammy always thought she was so fucking smart. She just knew she was smarter than everyone else. Little did she know, I was just as smart as her, if not smarter than her. She was always so busy listening to that miserable old crazy bitch. That heffa always thought was better than me. Sure she made more money and had bigger business moves than me, but what she didn't realize is that there was always a method to my madness and calculation in all of my chaos. She thought I was some young, dumb broad she could boss around forever, but I've been patiently waiting for this moment since the moment I met her. I just relaxed and waited for this moment where I would be able to taste the sweet revenge after all of these fucking years. She sincerely thought I was just her sidekick," she said as she fell into a fit of laughter. "Well, Tanya Isabella is nobody's sidekick, and that bitch is gone learn about me today!"

| 8 |

Get it Together, Tammy

"Damn, you really are good at your craft," Rasheeda said as she admired her make-up and hair in the mirror. "I'm glad Jordan practically forced me to go through with this," she said with a giggle. "For real though, my bad for the really rough introduction. Most of these hoes are just so disrespectful. I've been with his ass since I was only 14, and these bitches be acting like I ain't wifey."

"I hear you, girl, cause I've been there too, but case and point, you can't jump on every female. You're cute, and as long as you keep playing your position and doing what you've been doing to keep him around, you won't have to worry about what these other broads are doing. Remember," Tammy said as she started packing her stuff up. "These thirsty hoes are dying for attention, so don't feed them with what they're looking for."

"Yeah, you're right about that,"Rasheeda exclaimed. "Fuck these dusty birds. You know you seem really smart and cool, so why the hell are you hanging around with bum ass Tanya," she asked.

Tammy let out a chuckle before she responded. "I really wish I knew why everyone kept saying things like that about her, but I don't want to get into it right now since she isn't here to defend herself."

"I respect the loyalty because that's rare to see anymore, but fuck that and fuck her. She's a liar, a thief, and will sleep with your man in a heartbeat. You really shouldn't trust that broad. Anyway," Rasheeda said as she took out a crisp fifty-dollar bill to tip Tammy. "My man's cousin is coming back into town, so I'm going to get his number and give it to you. I just have this feeling that you two will really hit it off."

"I don't know," Tammy said skeptically. "I just don't think I'm ready to jump into anything with anybody right now."

"Nobody said you had to marry his ass," Rasheeda laughed. "Just go out for some drinks and keep him and my nigga away from each other for a while. If you do that for me, then I'll make sure to keep you flooded with business."

When she heard the sound of money, Tammy replied the only way she could. "Ok then," she said, "Set it up."

***

I hate blind dates. If it wasn't about the money, I wouldn't have even agreed to this. Tammy thought to herself as she walked up to the restaurant where she was meeting Jordan's cousin. *I can't believe I let Rasheeda talk me into this.*

Tammy took the number that Rasheeda have given to her and decided to just use it anyway.

She and Rick would have endless conversations; And he seemed to possess the one trait that Tammy longed for in a partner – immeasurable intelligence. They talked about everything from music to politics and everything else in between. Tammy considered herself to be very knowledgeable, but found herself having to look up things after conversing with him because she had never met a man that was so smart.

If anything, I can just take away a friend out of this because I'm sure with my luck he can't be smart and good looking. There is just no way.

Tammy finally made it to the restaurant and was completely surprised at what she saw. She didn't immediately walk to the front door because she wanted to try to figure out which one was him before he had a chance to see her.

Lord, if he is the tall, super fine one, I promise I'll try to get my life together. Just please let him be the fine one, Tammy silently prayed.

She pulled out her cellphone and dialed his number. She never once moved her eyes from the 6'6", caramel mocha man whose stature and presence was unable to miss even through the crowded city streets.

The man she had been secretly admiring looked up in her direction and their eyes met. Then, he answered his phone and she heard the sweet, familiar voice she had grown to enjoy talking to coming from the most attractive man she had ever laid her eyes on. He smiled a beautiful smile with a set of perfectly straight, white teeth and it caused Tammy's heart to melt.

Get it together Tammy, she coached herself as she walked to the restaurant's entrance to meet him. *You don't act like this for men because they are supposed to act like this for you.*

Tammy was always super confident and it was a trait that seemed to drive men wild for her. For the first time ever, Tammy felt completely off of her game as she tried her best to play it cool, but the butterflies dancing around her stomach made it nearly impossible to just remain calm.

"Good evening beautiful," he said as he leaned in to lightly embrace her and kiss her on the cheek.

Oh my gosh he smells so good too. He's fine, smart, and he can dress. Thank you Jesus, she thought as she returned his embrace.

"Good evening handsome," she replied unable to contain the grin she was wearing.

"You are not at all what I expected," he said as he softly grabbed her hand and opened the door to let her inside the restaurant.

They grabbed a booth in the small, cozy sports bar that Tammy suggested that they meet at. Tammy loved sports and would frequently come because the owner would always address her by name and even served her alcohol even though she wasn't at the legal age to drink yet. She hated the idea of dressing up super fancy, and she was thrilled to know that he was just as excited to just drink beers and watch the game as she was.

They talked about everything from the game that they were watching to the last book they had a chance to sit and read. The evening was filled with lots of smiles, laughter, and endless conversation.

After the game was over and the establishment began to clear out, he paid for their tab as they both got ready to leave.

"The night is still so early," he said as he checked his watch. "Come with me," he gently grabbed Tammy's hand and led her to his vehicle. Tammy usually would never have just gone off with a man she didn't know that well, much less a man she just met for the first time, but for the first time in her life, she had finally met someone she thought a man was supposed to be.

***

"Ma, he's perfect," Tammy gushed as she laid back on the couch while Ms. Cruz made them lunch. "He's tall like I like my men. He's gorgeous, and has the most amazing smile. I could talk about that smile forever, but my God, he's like the smartest human I've ever met. I could -,"

"Could you please shut the hell up," Ms. Cruz interjected. "You've been here for all of an hour, and you can't seem to stop talking about this guy. Who the hell are you, and what the hell have you done with Tammy," she asked as she looked over at Tammy from the kitchen's doorway.

"I know," Tammy replied with a girly giggle. "I've never been like this with anyone. Even when I did date those guys before him, I was always stuck in my ways, but something about him is just so different. He's a businessman and unlike any of these wanna-be trap stars that get at me every day. Maybe it will feel nice to just be courted by a real gentleman instead of playing mind games with these idiots."

"Be careful, amor," Ms. Cruz warned as she took her seat next to Tammy. "This is the first time I've ever seen you like this with anyone. Don't rush it and take your time. The crazy thing is, you took an engagement ring from a man, and I hardly heard you talk about him. Now, you can't stop gushing over this random guy. I know it's going to be hard, especially with you being so infatuated already. Gradually let him in, please. I don't want to see you get hurt."

"I went with him to meet some of his business partners after dinner last night," Tammy said as she sat up, completely ignoring what Ms. Cruz was saying.

"You did what," Ms. Cruz yelled as she slammed her fist on the coffee table. "Haven't I taught you better than to be a cheap whore by going home with someone? Tammy, you hardly know the man. What the hell were you thinking?"

"I know. I know, but our chemistry was just so strong. I've never met anyone who gave me butterflies like that before. I didn't kiss him or anything like that. I still remained a lady, but I was just curious to see what would happen. I know what I'm doing," Tammy said. "I still got this."

"I sure hope so," Ms. Cruz pleaded."

***

It was 12:05 AM, and Tammy hadn't heard from Rick since they went on their date almost four nights ago. Just as Tammy finished wrapping her hair and climbing into bed, she saw the text come in from the man she had wanted to talk to since the first night they met.

"Hey beautiful, I've been really busy lately. Why don't you come over," his text read.

Although Tammy wanted to just throw on a cute fit, light natural make-up, and a cute hairdo, she had to keep her cool. Instead, she just responded, "I know a man of your stature is not used to hearing no, so instead, I'll just have to politely decline. In the future, please remember that I'm a lady, so contact me at a decent hour or not at all. Have a good night."

***

"Ugh," Tammy huffed. "I kept my cool, and I laid down the law, but I was nice and respectful. It's been almost two weeks since I've heard from him. I play these games with people," she growled. "I do not get these games played with me."

"I told you to just take it slow," Ms. Cruz said. "Karma's a bitch, and you do realize that you'll eventually have to pay for those hearts you've played with through all of these years."

"It's not like I do it on purpose," Tammy snapped back. "I'm just me, and men seem to love it. I'm not loving or affectionate, and I'll probably never be. For some reason, guys seem to just eat it up. Why is he not doing the same thing? Does he not know who the hell I am?"

"Oh, please shut the fuck up," Ms. Cruz interjected. "I love you, but you really act like you're the best thing since sliced bread. I've been teaching you things all of these years because I want you to learn from my mistakes, but you've used them for your own selfish reasons. It's a shame that you're so smart yet so dumb at the same damn time.

Can I be honest with you, sweetie? It's actually kind of funny watching you pace back and forth and practically pull your hair out over this," Ms. Cruz said as she tried to hold back a chuckle. "You seem to forget that even though you are smart, there are people out there that are smarter than you. You put yourself on this high-ass pedestal. Now that you're not receiving the amount of attention you usually claim to hate, you don't know what to do with yourself.

Now you see exactly how it feels to be knocked flat on your face. The bible teaches you to remain humble, but you choose to be a bitch about every damn thing," she said bluntly. "You need to learn to learn to be more modest and humble yourself."

"I don't need to do anything but make my money and die," Tammy responded with a slight attitude before she turned on the television. She wanted to drown out the sounds of the advice she had heard a thousand times from her mother, father, stepfather, and Ms. Cruz several times before but always hated to hear.

"Ok, Tee," Ms. Cruz started. "I forgot you know everything there is to know about everything. What the hell could I possibly know about life? I just happen to be an old lady who dated and made millions of dollars with an international drug dealer while traveling the world and meeting different people. Obviously, you don't want my advice, so I won't give it to you anymore. You can trust and believe, though, that what you don't hear, you will feel."

| 9 |

Lose My Number

"Did you like the sneakers and clothes I bought for you," Derrick asked over a meal. It had been a while since they had spent any real time together, so he wanted to treat her to a fancy dinner.

"Yeah, they were all nice and fit perfectly. Thank you," Tammy replied nonchalantly.

"What's wrong with you yo," he asked with much concern as he watched Tammy play around in her food instead of gobbling it up like she normally would have.

Those around Tammy could instantly tell when something was bothering her. Although she claimed to not care most of the time, Tammy undeniably wore her heart on her sleeve. Whenever she was upset, the talkative know-it-all would go eerily silent or not eat, both of which were entirely out of her character.

"You've been acting mad funny ever since you came back. For some reason, I really thought that when you moved up here, things would finally change between us."

"What are you talking about," she asked, clearly aggravated as she dropped her fork into her plate. "I never sold you any dreams or told you to expect anything from me," she said as she sat back in the chair she was sitting in and folded her arms.

"Look," he started. "I'm not trying to piss you off because it's evident that you're already in a bad mood, but I just don't know how to win with you.

I've been chasing you for years. I've wined and dined you. I've spent thousands of dollars on gifts, jewelry, purses, and shoes. Anything that you want, I make it happen for you. Why wouldn't you want a man in your corner whose only concern is to make you smile? Every time I try to bring up the possibility of us, you get pissed off instead of realizing that I really care and want to be with you."

Tammy took a deep breath before she responded. "You don't love me," she started as she sat up and leaned in closer to him. "You only care about your fucking ego because you've finally met someone who is not dying to get in bed with you because of that cute smile or the fact that you like to break bread. Once you've felt like you've got me like you've got those other girls, you'll be on to something else, so please spare with the mushy feelings and shit."

The confused look on Derrick's face was an immediate giveaway that he did not like the response he had just received about his feelings.

"How the fuck are you going to tell me how I feel," he snapped, causing the other patrons in the restaurant to turn and look at the young couple who were obviously quarreling.

He took a second to regain his composure before he started speaking again. "I don't do half of the shit I do for you for these bum ass females around here. The only reason I even deal with them still is because you've always been on this bullshit. I'm no trick, and ten times out of ten, I'm not breaking no money for a female and especially not one who ain't even my chick.

I don't press you about shit besides what's going on between us because one day you seem into me, and the next day it's like I don't even exist to you. If you're hurt because you chose to deal with some bum ass niggas in your past, then you should take that up with a therapist instead of taking it out on me. Otherwise, just be honest with me and let me know how much money you're really expecting me to drop before you lose this crazy-ass attitude that you got."

"Ha," Tammy exclaimed, once again causing those around them to turn their attention to the two of them. She leaned in even closer and softly but with much authority spoke. "You've clearly got me fucked up Derrick, so let me fix this shit for you.

I do not *need* you or any other nigga for that matter. I could give two shits about those raggedy-ass dollars that you spend because I make more than what you've spent on me daily, so let's be serious here. Anything that you think you can do for me, I can do even more by my damn self. I can't believe that you played yourself thinking that I was only keeping you around because you buy me shit every now and then," she pulled her wallet out and peeled three crisp twenty-dollar bills to cover her meal and the tip. She placed the money in the center of the table and hung her purse on her shoulder.

"Time is money, and clearly, the time I've invested with you through all of these years is sadly going to be a waste for me. Just for future reference, bread attracts birds and not women like me, so you're free to do what you want with whoever you chose. I'm no longer wasting my time with something that's clearly going nowhere. You're so ungrateful for the time I spent opening up and getting to know you. Sorry, I'm not like the rest of the hoes you attract that just wants to be easily available to you. Clearly, you deserve those bitches that everyone else is always passing around on the block."

Tammy stood up and got ready to leave. "Don't worry about taking me home. Lord knows, the last thing I need is for you to have another thing to hold over my head that you've done for me. I can use *my* own money to get *my* own cab, so I have *my* own way home. The only thing I need you to do now is to lose my number."

***

"You're such an asshole," Tiffany said when she could finally stop laughing so hard as the story Tammy had just told the three sisters.

Tammy didn't feel like going home immediately after her incident with Derrick. She also hadn't been to see Ms. Cruz's for almost three weeks, so she just decided to lounge around with Tanya and her sisters for the rest of the night.

"Damn, so you finally let Derrick go back on the market," Tanya asked. "That means he's free game since you clearly don't want him, right?"

Tammy made a mental note at just how excited she seemed to be about her recent squabble with Derrick. *I remember Rashee•a sai• that Tanya woul• cross someone for a man, but woul• she seriously •o that to me? Please, let everyone else be wrong about Tanya. I refuse to believe someone I consi•er such a close frien• coul• actually be someone who woul• plot behin• my back.*

"I never said I didn't want him in my corner anymore," Tammy corrected her. "I put him exactly where I wanted him. This man has been trying to get at me for four years already and has never even gotten a kiss from me. Do you really think that a man with that large ego is going to let all of his hard work go in vain? He'll be back, and he'll be giving and spending more than ever because now I'll convince him that all of this is all his fault."

"You're such an evil bitch," Tanya replied with a heinous laugh.

| 10 |

She Lied to You, But She Played Me Too...

Isabella's tone and demeanor had calmed down, and her voice became soft once more.

"She lied to you, but worst of all, she played me too. She and I were supposed to be friends forever, and I never expected her to act this way with either one of us.

Shit, me and Tammy have been rocking and running the streets together since we were kids. Now, all of a sudden, she wants to act like I haven't always had her back through every fucking thing. She was supposed to be my friend and I'm not sure why she's all of a sudden switching up on me like something has changed. Either way, I'm going to get to the bottom of it."

K.Y. was beginning to get sick of Isabella's mood swings, but he just had to find out how much she knew. One minute, she seemed ready for revenge. The next, she was venting like she was hurt about the status of her relationship with Tammy. Something told him that he shouldn't trust any of them at this point. Regardless of what his better judgment was warning him, now, he had way too many questions that he desperately needed to be answered.

"Ok," he said, finally speaking up. "I hear you that she fucked us over, and now it's beginning to finally look that way to me.

All this time, I thought Ra had used you to get close to me so that he could rob me blind, and now learning that you and Tammy were actually friends tells me there is a whole lot of shit that I really don't know."

"You really thought your dumb ass friend was capable of something as sneaky and manipulative as this," Isabella asked with a laugh. "That stupid ass nigga couldn't even follow the rules we tried to set up for him to keep him off of everyone's radar. His dumb ass was too eager to use the little bit of money that he was making to impress everyone around him. Let's not talk about his ability to not get high off of his own supply. Everyone knows that that is rule number one in this fucking game. That nigga stays using all of his own shit."

It shocked K.Y to hear the truth. Of course, for a moment he thought that Rashard had been stealing from him. After all, where would the money he was making have come from? He never knew Rashard to have large amounts of cash, even when he was running the streets together with Kyle.

"I know it sounds crazy," he responded. "But after my shit came up missing the first time, I had my suspicions. I saw him living lavishly and blowing money like crazy. The only story that would have made sense was that he stole the large amounts of cash from me."

Once again, Isabella fell into a rage of laughter. "Well damn," she said once she finally caught her breath. "I guess home girl is way better than I give her credit for because she managed to convince you that someone you've known most of your life was capable of crossing you. She broke your heart, took your money and product, and managed to turn you against the only real friend you probably ever had. That bitch is real good at painting pictures for what she wants other people to see."

Something about her last comment made K.Y become enraged. Maybe it wasn't Isabella's fault, but she wasn't innocent either. It bothered him to hear her laughing at him during his painful time when her confused ass seemed to be just as hurt about her friend's rejection.

"Enough with the fucking riddles," Kyle said sternly. "One minute you want to talk about how long ya'll have been friends, and the next second you're screaming out your full government name like niggas was supposed to be familiar with who the fuck you are. Can we just get to the shit that matters here? Are you going to give me the answers I'm looking for, or do you want to continue playing this innocent card like I shouldn't hate your guts too?"

"Meet me at our usual spot at 9:00 PM tomorrow, and I'll tell you everything that you want to know. Just remember, you're not running shit this time. The last time I trusted you to follow through with your words, you played me too. Don't forget that you've done shit to me too that made playing you easy as fuck," Isabella responded before she ended the call.

| 11 |

Is There Anything You Can't Do

"Is there anything that you can't do," Rasheeda asked as she admired the acrylic nails Tammy had just done for her. "It's like you are almost incapable of disappointing someone." She took another moment to enjoy her nails before correcting herself. "Well actually, you did disappoint me with my boy. What the hell happened between you two?"

The thought of Rick instantly brought unwelcomed butterflies to Tammy's stomach.

"Girl please," Tammy responded. "I'm a grown-ass woman who does not have time for games. It seems like that is all your boy is about."

Rasheeda chuckled. "That's funny because when I asked him about you, I got a similar answer. It sounds like you two have some kind of disconnect, and you're both too stubborn to make the first move. You should call him. What do you have to lose?"

"Hell no," Tammy bellowed. "If he wants to deal with me, he also has my number."

"Ugh," Rasheeda replied with pure disgust. "Me, my boo, a couple homies, and Rick are going to go to the spot to watch the game. The least you can do is come through and casually run into him. All you have to do is play it off like you didn't know he was going to be there tonight."

Tammy thought about it briefly. She didn't want to be the one to make the first move because that was something she never did. At the same time, she couldn't stop thinking about Rick, and she didn't want to miss the opportunity to try with him again.. *I do want to see Rick. Tonight will also be an opportunity to use him to put Derrick exactly where I want because I know he is going to be there tonight too. It would be like killing two birds with one stone.*

***

Tammy sat at the booth with Rasheeda and her homegirls while anxiously waiting for Rick to arrive. She quickly scanned across the bar, hoping to see Rick before he saw her. She didn't find what she was looking for, but she was surprised at what she did see. A few tables over, she noticed a man wearing his hat low and hoodie staring directly at her. As soon as her eyes locked with his, he quickly looked away.

Usually, she would have shrugged it off as another admirer, but Tammy had seen this man before. In fact, as she thought more about it, she had seen him several times. Because he looked young, she always assumed that his presence was a mere coincidence, but this time it didn't feel that way to her. Something in her gut told her she needed to get some answers.

She had noticed him for the fourth time that week and finally wanted to get to the bottom of his continuous presence.

She got up and took a seat right across from the man at his table.

"This is the fourth time I've seen your face staring at me in only five days. Why," Tammy asked sternly.

"I don't know," he responded. "Maybe you're stalking me," he replied dispassionately.

"Or maybe it's the other way around," she spat back. "I see you more often than I should. What's your name, and who do you work for?"

Tammy was no fool. She knew what her father did for a living, and she knew she always had to keep her eyes and ears open.

"Ma'am, I don't know what you're talking about. Can you please go back to your friends now? I'm just trying to relax and enjoy my evening."

Although his demeanor was cool and relaxed, Tammy wasn't buying it.

"Cut the shit," she said as she slammed her fist on the table. "This week alone I've seen you at all of my hang-out spots. Last week I caught you in front of my building three times, and a month ago I peeped you by my grandmother's house. You better tell me who sent you, why, and fast, or I'll have this place so hot I'll melt your black ass to that leather seat you're sitting in." Tammy threatened, letting him know she would call her father to have him handled immediately.

"Just chill," the man said as he held his hands up.

"I will not. Not until you tell me who the hell you are," she said as she slid her cell phone out of her pocket.

Not wanting his boss to know that his cover had been blown, the man thought it was best for him just reason with her.

"If you can agree to keep this conversation between you and I, then I will tell you what you want and leave you alone for the rest of the night," he responded.

He sat there silently, hoping she would accept his offer. Unfortunately for him, Tammy didn't agree to his deal, but he knew he would hear her mouth whether he answered her or not. He had heard and witnessed the terrible wrath of Tammy but knew the wrath he was going to experience if she made the call was going to be much worse than what she could ever do to him.

Jason slightly pulled back his hoody so she could better see his face. "Lino asked me to keep an eye on you," he confessed.

"What? Why," she asked, clearly confused. "Is everything ok with my father?"

"He's fine," he responded.

"So then why are you keeping tabs on me like I'm a baby or something?"

“I’m doing it because it’s my job," Jason responded. "I’ve been doing this since you were practically born. I’m actually surprised it took you this long to notice me. Unlike you, your mother was always aware of her surroundings. She could spot one of Lino’s men even in a crowded place larger than this. That woman was always on point. She knew what she was dealing with.”

She wasn’t sure if it was the fact that an unknown man had mentioned her mother or if it was because he had openly admitted to following her for years, but his statement really upset Tammy.

“Fuck you! I always know what’s going on around me. I don’t need some fake ass thug with no real life or job clocking me or my every fucking move,” she spat back.

“Obviously, you do,” Jason responded as he leaned in close to her and speaking with much authority. “What your father does is dangerous as hell, and you parlay around here like shit is sweet. Your every move is predictable as shit because you go to the same damn places with the same motherfuckers using the same routes all the fucking time! You’re lucky niggas know Lino keeps a set of eyes on you at all times, or someone would have snatched your ass up years ago.”

Tammy didn’t respond. Her mother had always told her stories of the hate she had for always being watched and followed when she and Lino were together. Tammy had hoped that since she never saw her father conduct business, he had gotten out of the game for good.

“I know everything there is to know about you just from watching you for so long. You better chill your ass out before you find yourself in some serious heat. I know you’re not fucking with that little nigga Derrick right now, but knowing how you move, he’ll be back in once he drops the right amount of cash. If you’re as smart as I think you are, you will cut that nigga off once and for all. You don’t need guys like him in your corner. All money is not good money,” Jason declared as he sat back in his seat.

“Fuck you and your opinion of me and what I do. I know what the hell I’m doing, so you need to fall back and mind your damn business. Anyway,” she said as she lowered her hostile tone. “I don’t lose sleep over the thoughts of people, especially not one with a shitty ass job like you have. You can't have a life when you're so busy worried about me and mine," Tammy spat back.

"You should be happy that I'm so involved in what you got going on instead of just acting like some hateful, ungrateful bitch," he said flatly. Tammy's eyes got wide, and she instantly became more enraged than she had been just moments before.

"You dumb ass, crusty lip having, bum ass motherfucker should be the last one calling anyone a bitch. I can promise you that you haven't seen a bitch until you've really pissed me off, and you are almost there," Tammy stated.

"Oh please," he retorted with a chuckle. "You can save that fake shit for your bum clowns you deal with, but that shit doesn't scare me. I've earned my respect out here, so I don't care if I don't have yours. You don't have to believe me because I don't lose sleep over the opinions of others, especially not one with a shitty know-it-all attitude like you," he said, mocking her.

"I'm going to keep up with my end of the bargain. I'll leave you alone for the rest of the evening, but now you'll see just how important my job really is," Jason chuckled. "Keep your eyes and ears wide open. You have no idea how much you would cost in these streets to the right motherfucker. Oh," he said as he stood up. "Don't think telling Lino is going to get me off of your back either. Yeah, he'll probably fire me or curse me out, but someone else will just be in my spot the moment I leave. You'll have a different man following you around all the time, and you may not be lucky enough to find someone who cares about your safety like I have grown to."

Although Tammy never realized she had security before, it suddenly made her nervous knowing that her usual protection was not going to be around to protect her. Still, she refused to let him know that.

"Have fun," Jason said. "Call me when you're leaving if you want me to follow you home like I always do. You know these streets are ruthless, and one hair off of your pretty little head is worth a lot to a nigga looking to come up. "

"I don't want you to do shit but get a real-life and leave mine alone," Tammy spat coldly.

"Aight, but you can't say that I didn't warn you." Jason slid her his number and left.

As he said, the man got up and left without incident. Tammy took a deep breath as she allowed his words to finally soak in. At that moment, she made a mental note to start paying more attention to her surroundings and learning more about what her father was still up to.

Tammy scanned the room again, and noticed Derrick playing pool with one of his hoes by the pool table close to the bar. He saw her, and to her surprise, he didn't acknowledge her and went back to his game. Not one to be phased by his rude gesture, she turned her attention to the game that was playing.

She continued scanning the room, and a few tables over, she found what she had been looking for. The sight of Rick laughing with a few of his boys brought a smile to her face that she could not hide. He must have felt her adoring eyes boring a hole in his mouth as she melted at the sight of his infectious smile all over again. Rick put his beer down and gave her a sly grin before making his way to where she was.

"Well, hello, stranger," Rick said as he took his seat. "I guess you're too good to pick up the phone to check on your friends now?"

"I guess you forgot that a phone works both ways, amigo," Tammy responded, matching his sly grin.

"Yeah, you're right about that," he chuckled. "I won't front because you crossed my mind a few times while you took your hiatus. It's cool though, I can respect a busy woman."

"Oh, please don't blame this lacuna on me," she replied. "I guess you're not one to handle hearing no. I declined your late-night invitation and never heard from you again."

"Your mouth is real fresh," Rick snickered. "I like it, though."

The two caught up for lost time and completely forgot about the company they had both arrived with and the game. Several times throughout the evening, she had noticed Derrick staring on in envy.

Still, she played it cool and didn't acknowledge the fact that her plan was clearly working.

After two hours of laughing, drinking, and having a good time, he interrupted Tammy while she was in the middle of telling him about the last book she had read.

"Let's just get out of here," he interjected. "I want to go somewhere more quiet and relaxed, so I can pick your brain some more."

"Sir, what kind of woman do you take me for," she asked, half-joking. "You're lucky that I find something about you absolutely irresistible, and I do enjoy a good mind fuck every now and then," she replied as she grabbed his hand and once again followed him out.

***

"Oh my gosh," Tammy gushed as she and Ms. Cruz sat on the stoop in front of Ms. Cruz's building. "He's just so perfect, ma!"

"You left with this man again," Ms. Cruz asked in disgust. "You're obviously losing your touch."

"Come on now," Tammy reasoned. "What's wrong with me not wanting to treat him the same way I've treated men before him? He acts different, so why not treat him different?"

"What the hell is so different about a man you just met? You're used to men wining and dining you, and what has this one done for you?"

"It's not about what he can give to me cause I can get stuff myself or get someone else to give it to me, but it's just all in the way he makes me feel. Last night he took me out for sushi. He actually persuaded me to try something new, and you know how picky I am with my food. We sat in the park underneath the stars feeding each other food that was so foreign to me. We never once stopped talking or laughing. We never have the same conversations, and we never do the same things. I feel like I could talk to him for hours, and I always learn something new from him. It's all just different and exciting," Tammy gushed.

"It's always that way, in the beginning, mi amor. It sounds to me like you're falling for this man and fast. I remember feeling that exact way once about my sweet Lorenzo."

Tammy had waited for years to hear Ms. Cruz go into more detail about the man that could stir some passionate emotions out of Ms. Cruz. "I didn't understand at the time what he was saying to me, but the way the dialect rolled off of his beautiful lips made me immediately melt. I had always been so headstrong, direct, and full of attitude with men that it was weird to finally meet someone who made me want to know them.

He made me want to open up to him without ever forcing me or pulling me out of my comfort zone. He let me be free and just be me. He didn't try to control me or anything I said or any move I made. I was free. I knew what he did for a living, and at the time, I hated it. After learning why and watching how what he did made a difference in the lives of so many, I learned to respect his hustle which allowed me to respect him even more. He was caring, giving, and loving, but he kept that part reserved for me. I knew that there was another side to him. It was like he was two different people trapped in one body.

Most people knew Lorenzo as the take-no-bullshit businessman, but some knew he was a gentle giant in how he looked out for those around him. No matter what, though, he always kept that super sweet Lorenzo just for me when no one else was around." She took a deep breath and stopped speaking for a moment. "I'll love that man as long as I live," she said as she broke out of the slight trance that retelling her story had her in. "Anyway, mi amor, I'm happy that you seemed to finally find love, just please be careful."

***

Tammy and Rick had become inseparable. They were all over the city and had visited different museums, restaurants, and exhibits.

After meeting Jason two months ago, Tammy did her best to switch up her routes and schedule to make it nearly impossible for him to find her or keep tabs on her every move. For the last month and a half, Tammy and Rick had been staying in a lovely suite in Upper Manhattan as a small get away from their typical day-to-day operations.

Even though Tammy hadn't had a chance to see Ms. Cruz in the last few weeks since she had been spending so much time with Rick, she always made sure to stay in constant communication with her.

Rick had to get back to work, and Tammy didn't feel like hanging out alone, so she thought she would go back to Brooklyn for the day and hopefully avoid Jason.

Tammy was halfway up the stoop that led to Ms. Cruz's apartment when she heard an angry, deafening tone call out her name. Without turning around, she knew exactly who it was and that her quick trip unnoticed was unsuccessful.

"What the hell are you thinking disappearing on me like that," he howled with much aggravation. "Do you have any idea how hard it is to tell Lino that I had no update on his only daughter when watching you has been my only job for the last two fucking decades?"

"Look," Tammy started before he sharply cut her off.

"I don't want to hear it," he exploded. "Looking out for you when you would rather be stubborn to make my job harder is inexcusable and unacceptable. I don't want to hear shit you have to say about it. You're so busy running around thinking you're grown, and you have no idea what kind of shit you've stepped in or caused."

Hearing all of the commotion through her open window caused Ms. Cruz to come down to see what all the excitement was about.

"Beast stop this foolishness in front of my damn house," Ms. Cruz ordered sternly.

"My bad, ma," Jason responded to her demand. "I'm cool now."

Tammy wore a confused look on her face as she looked between Jason and Ms. Cruz.

Ms. Cruz was the first one to break the awkward silence. "Bring your two crazy asses in this damn house, ahora."

The two of them did as they were told and followed Ms. Cruz upstairs. Once they were all locked in her house, Tammy erupted with the questions she had been dying to know.

"How the hell do you two know each other, and why the fuck is he calling you ma?"

"First of all," Ms. Cruz spoke. "I'm not one of your little friends, so remember to talk to me with nothing but respect.

I never held back the fact that your father and I used to work together, so naturally, I'm going to know some of his other employees. Beast has been working for your dad since he was a tiny boy who probably couldn't even piss straight," Ms. Cruz said with a giggle.

"He and I had a few missions together, but he was always security. If you ever needed some protection, everyone knows that Beast is definitely the best of the best."

Tammy stood there stunned. Although Ms. Cruz had admitted to working with Lorenzo and her father, Tammy always had a hard time believing someone as small and frail as Ms. Cruz could have been mixed up in such dangerous work.

Ms. Cruz was an older woman, and it was obvious from the stories that she would tell that she was at least 65 years old. Still, whenever Tammy would ask about her age, she would always remind her that a *real* lady never reveals the truth.

No matter how old she was, there was no denying that Estrella Cruz was a problem in her prime. Even at her age, she was gorgeous and had clearly aged very well.

"Anyway, what is the reason for all of this carrying on," Ms. Cruz asked as she looked directly at Jason.

"She's so fucking hard-headed and stubborn. Her know-it-all attitude is going to get us both killed if she keeps this shit up," he barked.

"Tell me something I don't know," Ms. Cruz giggled.

"Well, this bum," Tammy said with much distaste, "has been stalking me and has been all up in my damn business."

"It's my fucking job," Jason screamed back at her.

In an effort to try to ease the tension growing in the room, Ms. Cruz spoke up again.

"Tamia Santiago, your father is a sweet yet very dangerous man who rubs elbows daily with other dangerous motherfuckers. These men out here know that the easiest way to get to your father is to go through his heart. We both know your dad is not a sentimental man, and a lot of it has to do with the kind of business he's in and the rest because he's reconditioned his mind to think like that.

Your mother hated this part of the game too, but Jason's job is way more important than you could ever imagine," Ms. Cruz continued. You are who you are; your father is who he is, and he does what he does. When are you going to just stop fighting it and embrace who you are and where you come from?"

Tammy huffed loudly because she realized that Ms. Cruz had finally made her point. She plopped herself down on the couch and folded her arms.

"Well, Ma, I hope this finally opens your eyes and answers your question as to why I hate drug dealers. This shit right here is exactly why I'll never fucking seriously date one."

"Well, you sure could have fooled the hell out of me," Jason said, finally speaking up again.

"Don't you ever get tired of making assumptions about someone you don't even know that well? What that hell is that supposed to mean anyway," Tammy asked him with much attitude.

"You're running around here like some lovesick kid with one of the biggest drug dealers on the east coast," he stated flatly.

"Oh please," Tammy chuckled. "I know all about how Derrick makes his chump change, and I hardly entertain him enough for you to even assume something as ridiculous as that. Anyway, he is most definitely nowhere near a kingpin status."

"Nobody was talking about lame-ass Derrick," Jason replied irritably. "Believe it or not, I been found out and caught on to the fact that you're running around all over town with the biggest drug dealer under your pops and my best friend, Patrick Bennett.

| 12 |

Leave Me the F*ck Alone

"I don't know anyone by the name of Patri-," as soon as the name started to roll off of her tongue, she placed two and two together.

"Patrick Bennett is the man that you've been gushing about like a love-struck puppy and going crazy over for the last few months," Ms. Cruz asked with large wide eyes. "Dios Mio, Señor," she said as she took a seat next to Tammy dazed in thought at the realization of the truth that had been exposed.

Tammy sat there confused as she watched Jason pace back and forth while Ms. Cruz prayed to God in Spanish, something she rarely did.

All Tammy could think about was how she had managed to fall for a man, much less so fast, who of all things was a drug dealer.

In the time she had been spending with him, she had completely opened up to Rick. She had told him some of her deepest and darkest secrets while letting her guard down and completely allowing herself to be free and naked for him. Without shedding a single piece of clothing, she had allowed him to get further inside of her than any man she had ever been physically intimate with. She managed to fall dangerously and passionately in love with his mind, which made everything about him even more desirable to her than he had been before.

She sat there completely bewildered. How had the only man she had ever let get into her heart and mind like that be the one thing she truly despised?

Once Ms. Cruz was done praying, she placed her arm around Tammy. Although Tammy hadn't said a word, she knew that she was hurt and confused. In all of the years she had known Tammy and through all of the conversations that they had had, she learned that Tammy had a very hard time showing emotions and letting others see the softer, more vulnerable side of her. Ms. Cruz was sure it came from the relationship she had witnessed and experienced from her own parents and stepfather, although Tammy had only talked about it briefly once.

***

"I always thought my mom and step pops hated me," Tammy said with a nervous chuckle. "My step pops never addressed me by my name, and he always just called me 'what's her name.' My mother used to beat my ass with anything and for anything. I got all of the beatings, and she would do it until she got tired, and my siblings would go off free.

They hated that I was so different and refused to conform to what they thought I should be.

I took care of myself and my family at all costs. Sometimes it required me to lie or manipulate others, but I never did it just for selfish reasons. They would enjoy the fruits of my labor but talk about me like a dog once it was all dead and gone.

They all hated the fact that I'm exactly like Lino. They said he was a liar, a manipulating user and that I would grow up to be just like him.

What was even harder about everything was growing up around so many damn rich white kids. I never heard of them getting the type of emotional, let alone physical, abuse I had to endure in my damn house. After I got too big for whoopings with baby dolls, extension cords, belts, spoons, hangers, and anything else in my mother's reach, I started getting straight punched in the mouth. She would punch me with all her might and then dare me to cry or hit her back. Who the hell does that?"

Ms. Cruz tried to explain that although what she lived in felt like abuse because of her immediate surroundings, Mariana was only parenting off of what she had learned from being raised in a third world country.

"Growing up in Honduras, you were only allowed to show two kinds of emotions." Ms. Cruz said as she tried to comfort Tammy from the painful memories she had shared with her. "You were either happy or mad. If you showed anything else, you were just a plain pussy. You couldn't let those around you find out your weak spots because then it made it easier for someone else to use it against you. It's hard to look at it positively now, but just think if you would have been raised by some soft pussy that allowed you to just cry like a baby all the time. You wouldn't be half as strong as you are now. You're as tough as you are now because you were raised by a strong-ass woman who instilled those same strong traits in you. I don't want to excuse what happened to you because it was abuse at the end of the day. One day you'll understand that your mom did the best she could with what she had at the time, even though all of it wasn't right."

***

Ms. Cruz desperately wanted to find the words to say to try to comfort Tammy now, but she didn't want to confuse her any more than she already was. If there was one thing that Ms. Cruz knew, a woman in love would do whatever she needed to do for that man. It doesn't matter what he does or what someone else says; the one in love had to make the best decision for them.

"I didn't have a chance to tell him yet because you guys have been so busy running around together. Either way, I thought it was time that at least one of you knew who you were dealing with," Jason said empathetically.

Tammy couldn't take sitting there anymore, allowing others to feel sorry for her as she wallowed in the pity of her poor judgment.

"I'll be back," she stated as she headed to the door.

"I'm going with you," Jason replied as he followed her direction.

"When will you just get off of my fucking back," she asked irritably. "Can't you see that I just need some alone time, and I don't want you breathing down my damn neck? Despite what you think, I'm a big girl and can handle shit on my own."

"When will you understand that outside of this being my job, I actually care about what happens to you? I'll stay out of sight and let you do your thing. I just need to make sure that you are protected while you're out here. Just because your dad is fine today doesn't mean shit can't go south if an opportunity arose from one of his enemies. I'm not trying to make shit harder for you, damn it. "

"Ugh," she roared as she held the door for him so that they could leave.

***

"I thought we were trying to get to know each other," Tammy screamed out to Rick when they were alone in the suite they had been shacking up in. "I told you almost everything there is to know about me and more, and you forget to mention the fact that you're a fucking drug dealer? How many nights did I sit here and utter my complete disgust for those who made their money that way?"

"I'm not trying to hear this shit or go through this with you, Tee," he replied back nonchalantly. "If you don't want to fucking deal with me anymore, then that's all you have to say."

It bothered Tammy to know that regardless of all of the time and energy they had spent trying to get to know each other, he could just walk away without an ounce of a fight. For once in her life, Tammy was on the other side of some of the games and mind tricks that she had played on other people.

"You're a selfish piece of shit that doesn't care about anyone or anything else. That's exactly why you do what the fuck you do and why the hell you're not even saying anything to try to get me to change my mind," Tammy said somberly.

"Tee, if there is one thing I've learned about you, I know that when your mind is made up, there is no use in trying to convince you. You have this idea that I'm anything else than what I've been showing you these last few months. I'm still me. I'm still the guy that just two nights ago you were professing your love to. I'm still the man who knows some of your darkest fears and desires. You've shared so many things with me in this short amount of time that I feel like I know you better than I know some people I've known my whole life.

Of course, I don't want you to just walk away, but I can't help it if you can't stay true to who you are and decide you want to fight it for the rest of your life."

Tammy was tired of hearing so many people tell her that she was not true to herself.

"Has no one ever taught you that we are brought to other people who are going to show us and expose us for what we really are," he asked. "Do you really think it was just some coincidence that you and I met? We meet who we are supposed to meet exactly when we are supposed to meet them. You're so busy being mad at me when in reality, the only person you're really mad at is yourself.

You're so busy denying who you are and what you really are that you're never taking away the lessons you're supposed to from the people that have been placed in your life for a reason. Stop fighting it and just embrace it."

"I don't want to hear any more of your bullshit," Tammy shrieked. "I'm not anything like you," she said with pure disgust dripping from her tone. "You're a liar and a fucking coward. You allowed me to know you, want you, and love you when you knew that-," before Tammy could finish her sentence, Patrick placed his arms around her and passionately kissed her lips. Tammy wanted to fight him, but everything about his embrace felt so right to her. She gave in to the softness of his touch and kissed him back lovingly.

Although being in his arms felt so good, Tammy couldn't stay out of her head long enough to truly enjoy the moment. Tammy was already confused before she got to the hotel, and the fact that the man who had her so hurt and perplexed was now filling her with lust and passion had her even more bewildered. The more she allowed herself to think about how she had allowed him to see places of her mind and soul, other men would have killed for a chance to catch a glimpse of, the angrier she became.

He was a hustler, and like her, he always had to be two steps ahead of his prey. He also had to know the master of perception and wordplay to conquer his target.

This man could have known who I was this entire time, she thought to herself as he softly rubbed his hands down her body and sat his hand gently on the small of her back. *How do I know he didn't sweet talk me just to get close to my father? Is this what Jason was trying to warn me about when he said there would be people trying to get to me to get to my father? How do I know he isn't trying to exploit the obvious weaknesses that I've shown him so quickly and foolishly? Was everything a lie? Did Rasheeda know what she was doing when she set us up? Am I the only one who has been feeling this feelings? Did he just get away with fucking playing me?*

Tammy was not an emotional person. She had no idea how to process the large amount of hurt, bliss, confusion, passion, and anger that she was feeling all at one time. It became too hard to try to fight the lump that was growing in her throat. Instead of submitting to crying, she lashed out with her anger instead.

She pushed him off of her. "Just get out of here and leave me the fuck alone. I never want to see your fucking face again. I hate you, everything about you, and everything you stand for."

Without another word, Patrick went into the bathroom where he had all of his things.

Tammy heard him ruffle through his stuff and assumed he was following the orders that she had just demanded. Although she had said she never wanted to see him, Tammy now couldn't imagine going a day without seeing that smile, hearing his laugh, or having him mind fuck her with their intense debates and conversations. She immediately became sad at the thought of not having him around but knew she could not admit it to him.

He stepped out of the bathroom with his large duffle bag of stuff and dropped it next to him on the floor. In his hand was a gold Magnum condom.

"Take your clothes off and get on the bed," he demanded firmly, clearly ignoring her previous requests.

"Who the hell do you think you are pressing me for anything, much less wanting sex from me," she asked him with much attitude.

"Did you hear what the fuck I just said," he replied as he took off his pants and placed the condom on his enormous penis.

Tammy had never seen him be so aggressive, and even though she was still so angry with him, she couldn't deny the fact that this side of him really turned her on. Instead of succumbing to his commands, she stood there, rolled her eyes, and folded her arms.

"You can leave now," she said flatly.

He kicked off his shoes and pants and went towards Tammy. He grabbed her arm with much more strength than he had held her with just moments ago.

"Why are you fucking holding me like that," she asked. "Are you fucking hard of hearing all of a sudden?"

"Why the hell are you so hard-headed? What the fuck did I just tell you to do? I'm not in the mood to say it again," he said as he stared intensely into her eyes.

Once again, she didn't give in to him and instead matched his fierce glare.

He threw her on the bed and forcefully ripped off the shirt she had been wearing. He unbuckled her belt buckle and pulled off her jeans as Tammy squirmed and made a weak attempt to fight off his effort to take off her clothes.

There was no denying that Patrick was much stronger than she was. Instead of tiring herself by continuing to fight him, she just laid there and allowed the tears she had been desperately fighting back to cover the nakedness she was now in.

He climbed on top of her and pushed her red Victoria Secret panties to the side.

"Do you really want me to stop," he whispered in her ear as he rubbed his hard dick against her warm, wet pussy. "I might be a lot of things, but a rapist damn sure isn't one of them. If I'm reading this situation wrong, just tell me, and I'll leave you alone for good."

Yes, she thought to herself in between sobs. She just couldn't bring her mouth to say what she was thinking. Sadly, he wasn't reading the situation wrong. Tammy loved rough sex, and no one had ever been as forceful with her as he was in this moment. Her body enjoyed everything he was doing to her. Her heart had finally felt something for someone it had never felt before. It was convincing her mind to follow the other parts of her that was presenting the problem.

"Get out of your head for one fucking minute, Tee. Stop fighting what the hell you're feeling. Don't tell me what your head is saying. Tell me what your body wants me to do. Tell me what's going to feel good to you right now," he said as his movements in her private area became faster and much more energetic. "I'm not perfect, and I never pretended to be. Regardless of my profession, I'm still everything you saw in me this morning. My dreams are still the same, and this passion that I have with you and for you doesn't change because of this shit I do to survive."

Patrick continued to rub his dick faster and faster on her clit. "I know sex isn't going to fix this mess. I don't expect it to. But we can enjoy each other in this moment and just agree to figure shit out as we go."

She didn't say anything, and the tears just fell faster and harder as she continued to battle herself in her mind. Something about figuring it out with him is all she wanted to do, but it felt impossible to shut off the millions of thoughts frantically running through her mind.

"Come on Tammy," Patrick continued. "You're the most outspoken motherfucker I know. If you continue to just lay here silently, I'm going to take it for the truth it is. You want me just as much as I want you right now. You're just afraid to admit it."

Tammy didn't respond. Instead, she grabbed her panties to move them more to the side to give him easier access. Patrick gently slid the head of his penis inside of her. She was tighter than he had expected. He made sure to enter her softly until he was all the way in. Once he was entirely inside of her, Tammy moaned at just how perfect he felt.

The way he moved his hips, it allowed him to hit spots that no one before him had touched. Originally, Tammy had just laid there almost emotionless as she tried to justify what she was thinking and feeling. But the more he stimulated her G-spot and how he seemed to know exactly when to go harder and deeper inside of her allowed her body to finally win the fight she was having with her mind. Tammy wrapped her arms around him and dug her nails in his muscular back as she wined her hips and matched his smooth rhythm until she violently came.

He pleased her body in many positions and would do it with such ease that he never once came out of her while he did it. He was gentle yet forceful, soft, yet passionate. For once in her life, Tammy was not in control of a situation and allowed herself to just enjoy what she was feeling.

They made love for hours, and once Patrick was satisfied with how he pleased her, he took a blunt he had rolled up from the night side table. He lit it, and after smoking it for a while, he handed it to Tammy.

Tammy used to smoke often with her friends but had calmed down considerably. Tammy already spent way too much time trapped in her mind trying to plan her next move that she came to the grasp that weed just wasn't her drug since it made it impossible to get out of her head when she was high. After the wild amount of passion that she had just had with Patrick, she didn't decline it like she usually would have and instead accepted his invitation. Tammy inhaled the smoke deeply and allowed it to fill her lungs. After holding it for a moment, she slowly allowed the smoke to escape her lips.

"I didn't say anything because I really liked the fact that you didn't know anything about me, what I did, or where I came from. Most females hear my name and automatically hear a come up," Patrick spoke up, breaking the silence. "I can't trust most women because I never know if they are dealing with me for the money or if they are just trying to set me up. I wanted you to know me for me because there is way more to me than the money I have and how I make it. I would have eventually told you, but for now, I just wanted to enjoy how naïve you were to that part of me."

Tammy didn't immediately speak up. There were so many things she wanted to say and so many questions she wanted him to answer. However, for now, she just wanted to enjoy the bliss she was feeling from the moment they had just shared. She had just enjoyed amazing sex with a man she was completely infatuated with. So instead of bombarding him with everything she wanted to know, the usually outspoken Tammy retreated to the one place that made her feel free and imprisoned her at the same time – her mind.

| 13 |

What the F*ck is That Supposed to Mean?

Damn, you just went completely ghost," Tanya said with much aggravation in her voice. "I haven't seen your ass in months, and the crazy part about it is that you live just a few blocks over. What the fuck have you been up to?"

After Patrick and Tammy made love in the hotel that they had stayed in for a month and a half, they stayed there for an extra month, enjoying the honeymoon phase of their relationship.

"I met someone," Tammy responded lovingly. "I've just been a little booed up and caught up with him."

"Hmm," Tanya replied unenthusiastically. "That sounds a little too mushy coming for a female who proudly claims that she'll be forever mackin.' Who the hell are you, and what have you done with my friend?"

"Well, things change," Tammy said in a matter-of-fact tone. Aren't you happy for me?"

"For what," Tanya asked irritably. "It will be over sooner or later, and then you'll remember where your real friends are. A real relationship isn't your style. You've tried it before, and you always leave once shit starts to get too deep. You might be trying to play him, or you might be trying to play yourself, but you won't play me."

"Damn, you sound like a real hater Tanya," Tiffany spoke up. "If a man can get Tamia Santiago to settle down, gush over him, and go ghost on her friends, he has to be special. Doesn't that mean something to you as her homegirl?"

"Settle down my ass," Tanya replied. "She is going to do his ass just like she's done everyone else she's ever been with. You know she is not letting go of any of her hoes just for one nigga. You all can play along with her and this foolishness, but I'm not buying it. Not even for a second.

Speaking of your hoes," Tanya said, changing the direction of the conversation. "Derrick has been desperately trying to get in contact with you. That nigga has even had his boy passing messages to me to try to get in contact with your ass. His boy just told me that D has been leaving all kinds of gifts, flowers, and shit at your pop's house. So I guess you were right; your plan actually did work."

"Fuck Derrick and that plan," Tammy responded. "I'm not even worried about all of that. I took a really long vacation, but now it's time to get back to the money. That girl Rasheeda has been keeping my calendar filled with all types of bitches wanting to get hooked up, and I put it off way too long.

Thanks to my dad, my beauty line will be out in the next few months, and it's time to just remind everyone that when it comes to anything beauty, Tamia Santiago is where it's at. I don't want to hear any more bullshit about Derrick or any of my old hoes. I just want to make my money and deal with my boo."

"Damn," the three sisters said in unison as they stared at Tammy in disbelief.

"I never thought I would see the day," Nina spoke up enthusiastically. "And if you like it, then I love it; I'm happy for your girl."

"Well, ya'll can play along, but I won't believe it until I see it for myself," Tanya spat back.

"He's going to be at our spot on Friday with some of his niggas to play a few games of pool and for a few drinks if ya'll want to meet him."

"Well I'm definitely going to be there too," Tanya said.

***

Tammy still didn't have a key to her father's house, so she always depended on whoever he left house sitting to let her in.

She knocked on the apartment door and was completely surprised to see Patrick when he opened the door.

"What the fuck are you doing here," he asked her softly and sternly. Instead of allowing her in, Patrick stepped outside and closed the door behind him.

"I should be the one asking you that question," Tammy replied as she tried to push her way into her apartment. "At least I actually live here."

"What do you mean you live here? Do you have any idea whose house this is?"

Tammy never told Patrick who her father was. She was far too gone into her feelings with Patrick to cut him out of her life, but she still had to protect her father just in case. She was hoping that in her silence he would say something that would prove he knew more about her than he was letting off.

They had talked about their families several times before, and she had always been honest about the kind of relationship she had with her father. She always felt that since it was unimportant for her to know his parents' names and occupations, it wasn't vital for him to know either.

"Lino is my father," Tammy declared as she avoided eye contact with Patrick.

"What the fuck," he whispered, hardly audible. "You got so pissed off with me for holding back secrets, and your secret is way bigger than mine."

"Well I just didn't think it was a big deal or something that you had to know right away. Like you, I wanted to bask in you being naive of whose daughter I was," Tammy responded.

"Oh, that's cute. You really think this shit is funny trying to mock some shit I said to you with a fucking smirk on your face. Tammy, it's a huge deal," Patrick responded as his voice got louder. "How do you just forget to mention that your dad and I deal with each other?"

"I really didn't think it was a problem, Rick. Now can I please get into my house," Tammy asked.

"Oh," he said with a chuckle. "You're the one that's had my runner going broke spending all of his fucking earnings on. I just can't believe this shit," Patrick huffed as he stood to the side to let her in.

"What's your problem," she asked "It's not like I'm dating him or fucking him. Derrick likes me, so he just buys me shit. Anyway, I had no idea ya'll were connected. Remember, you're the one who enjoyed the fact that I didn't know much about you."

"I don't care about what you do, it's not like I'm your man or anything like that," he responded flatly.

"What," Tammy asked him since she was clearly confused by his last statement.

"You heard me. You're free to do whatever the hell you want to do. It's not like you have to answer to me or anything."

"I'm a grown-ass woman," Tammy spoke up sternly. "I don't take orders or answer to anyone, not even Delino Santiago. I do not, however, share my body with guys that are not my man."

"I hear you," Patrick said with an attitude. "But I'm not always with you, so I don't know what you do with all of your time."

"What the fuck is that supposed to mean," Tammy asked. "I spend all of my free time with you."

"Exactly," he responded. "You act like that really helps you prove any fucking point. You spend most of your time with me because you don't have a job and you're not at least in school. You don't have shit going for yourself besides some fake ass hustle." He chuckled. "Who knows what else you do with the remaining hours of your day. Clearly, you got time to be selling niggas dreams, so they'll splurge on you. How the fuck am I supposed to buy some innocent role you're trying to sell me on?

I just want to make sure that I make it clear to you that you've got another thing coming if you think I'm going to support you or replace the financial spot of your father. I damn sure don't trick off on any female, so I will not be dropping no dollars on you like the rest of these niggas out here.

You really thought you were actually that much smarter than me, but you couldn't beat me even on my worst day. You've really lost your damn mind if you thought you were going to hustle money out of me or set me up."

Tammy was confused about how this conversation had gone so far south, but she didn't like the apparent shots he was throwing her way. She wasn't like most females, and he was not about to treat her like she was.

"I'm not one of these bum broads that you fuck with. I don't need you or your fucking money. I don't need you or my father to provide for me because I've been providing for my damn self since I was a jit. I only stay with my father since it's stupid for me to go live anywhere else. If I did, he would just end up paying someone for the added security, so why would I do that?

Look, if you want to act like a fucking dick head over who my father is, then fuck you and this damn conversation," Tammy thundered.

Jason had been in the house the whole time. He knew that something would eventually pop off once Patrick found out that Lino's precious little girl was the woman he had been dealing with. Despite being best friends for so long, Jason had a duty to protect Tammy and Lino, and he didn't want to get in the middle of their mess.

Tammy had begged him to keep her father's identity a secret until she figured out the perfect time to tell Patrick. It had been hard for Jason to support such a large secret from his very best friend, but he knew that breaking Tammy's trust could cost him his job or worst.

"Can you two get in here with all of this bullshit," Jason whispered as he poked his head out of the apartment door. "I think we all would agree that it would be best that less people knew you were having problems and all of the people involved."

Although they both were upset, they realized that what Jason was saying made a lot of sense.

"Beast, you better get your friend," she snapped loudly once they were inside the apartment.

"What," Patrick asked, clearly confused. "Yo J, I thought you were just supposed to be protecting the broad and not interacting with her and getting to know her personally. Wait," he said once the realization finally sat in that the two of them already knew each other. "Why the fuck didn't you tell me what was going on? If you were following her around, then you had to know that I was the nigga she was dealing with.

If you knew I was that nigga why didn't you say anything when I was laying around here talking to you about her? I can't believe you," Patrick said.

Jason took a deep breath before he started speaking. "I wanted to tell you, I really did, but I was asked to just hold this secret. It's nothing personal my guy. It's just business."

"I wanted to be the one to tell you this. I wanted to make sure that you were dealing with me for me and not because of who my father was," Tammy interjected. "I had no idea that when you found out, you were going to act like this."

"Why wouldn't I," Patrick shouted. "Do you have any idea who your father is or who I am? Do you not realize what the fuck we do for a living?"

"I realize that," Tammy responded. "That's why I didn't say anything to you. How was I supposed to know if you weren't just dealing with me because of who my father was? I know that this is a cutthroat game that my father is in, and I had to make sure he was protected too."

Not wanting to get any deeper into their obvious argument, Jason slid out of the apartment and decided to just wait downstairs until they were finished.

"You see, this is why I am the way I am. I'll forever remain a loner, and I won't ever need any fucking body. This whole time you had me thinking you were my partner, and you were just worried about you," Patrick replied back vengefully. "You want me to trust you and know that the person I'm dealing with is loyal, but the whole time you've been keeping a huge secret. How do you expect me to not feel like you might have just been trying to set me up to get me out of the game for good?"

"Are you fucking serious, Rick? I love you too much to –."

"Seriously, Tee, I don't want to hear it. I don't want to hear anything you have to say to me right now. You lied to me, plain and simple. At least a dozen times, I asked you what your issue with drug dealers was, and you never once told me it's because your father is one of the biggest drug dealers from here to the Caribbean. This man is known in so many states and countries for what he does, and you knew that and never said a fucking thing to me.

Not telling me is the same as lying to me, and certain things are just unforgettable," Patrick declared.

"So then what the fuck are you really trying to say to me," Tammy asked.

"I'm not trying to say anything. What I'm saying is that I can't deal with someone that I can't trust, and right now, I feel like I can't even trust you. You keep a secret like this, and you've got mad niggas in your camp already. I'm positive you won't miss one."

Without saying another word, he grabbed his keys off of the key hook and left. As much as Tammy wanted to stop him, her pride just wouldn't allow her to.

***

"What the hell," Tammy screamed out as she sat watched Ms. Cruz make lunch. "Does he not know who the hell I am? I'm a damn trophy, and I'm not going to be chasing around no fucking body. I don't give a shit who the hell he is. You know how many motherfuckers would kill for me to show them just a fraction of the love and attention I showed to his ass, and now he wants to give me his ass to kiss," Tammy huffed.

"Girl," Ms. Cruz started as she turned away from the arroz con pollo she was making. "Relax and sit your black ass down. I know I allow you to talk freely to me because I want you to understand that you are liberated and free to just be you, but you need to calm the hell out.

You better respect my damn house and recognize that no one is allowed to curse like that in this bitch besides this bitch," she said.

Even as upset as Tammy was, she could not fight the laughter that erupted from her.

"Can you please cut it out? I'm really mad for real, and you're in the mood to just joke and play around," Tammy said when the laughter finally ceased.

"That's your damn problem," Ms. Cruz said as she put the stove on low and joined Tammy at the kitchen table.

"You're always upset over some shit. You need to learn to chill the hell out and not take life or people so seriously. When it's all said and done, no one is making it out alive, so you need to cherish every moment and every person in your life while you have the chance to.

I know exactly why you're mad, but you just are not ready to admit it to yourself," Ms. Cruz said.

"Oh, really? If that's true, than what do you think I'm actually mad at?"

"You're mad at yourself. You know you should have told Patrick. Once you had a chance to hear his side and what he was feeling, you knew he was right. You're mad at yourself for being too prideful and stubborn that you just let him walk out of your life instead of doing something to change it. You're mad at the fact that you know he's so angry that he will not call you over this. You're also mad at the fact that you know in order to get back to where you were, you are actually going to have to be a bigger person and reach out to him first, and you're going to have to apologize.

You've been around way too long to not understand more about this game than you actually do. Trust takes so many years to build and just a second to lose, and the thing about trust is that once it is lost, it will never be the same again.

Like your father, Patrick has a job that the very men who work for him could be plotting to take everything he has worked so hard for. It's understandable that he would be suspicious of everyone he encounters, especially the woman he shares his bed and secrets with.

Tammy knew Ms. Cruz was right but hated to admit it. Tammy had always been stubborn, and the reason she worked out so well with the men she had dealt with before her is because they all realized that Tammy just was the way that she was. She was hard-headed and, worst of all, unapologetic.

"So you think I should say sorry to Patrick and just forgive all of the reckless talk he was saying to me," Tammy asked.

"Do you want to one day go to heaven," Ms. Cruz asked her instead of answering her question.

"Well, of course, I do," Tammy asked, confused. "What does that have anything to do with the question that I just asked you?"

"You can't expect to have mercy shown to you on judgment day when you're not willing to show it to other people. He talked to you sideways out of anger; that doesn't make his actions, okay, but you can certainly understand why. You're always so busy talking about being grown, but I'll tell you how to tell when you've really grown. When you can learn to remove yourself from a situation and recognize why someone potentially felt the way they did, and you care enough to make that right is how you can tell when you've actually grown. That proves that you're no longer the selfish brat that so many still make you out to be.

If you ever meant what you said when you told him that you loved him, you would do whatever you had to in order to make things right with him."

"I hear everything that you're saying, but I'm just not used to having to be the one that has to apologize or do anything to make it right. I'm just me, and typically I tell men that they can just leave me the hell alone if they don't like it. Nine times out of ten, though, they just do whatever they need to in order to stay in my good graces, and it really bothers me that he isn't like that. I've never had to work hard in any relationship, so I thought once I actually fell in love with someone that this whole thing would be easy."

"Well that's the problem right there! Love is never easy. A real relationship will require work from both sides each and every day.

Many people see this foolishness on T.V that these writers tell on love and everyone expects it to be a fairy tale romance story. Love is so hard because it is filled with pain that is needed to change so you can love someone selflessly. Relationships thrive on sacrifices and compromises because it's not enough to just say you love someone. You have to actually prove it with your actions.

If there is one thing that God hates, it is a prideful person because a prideful person is a useless person."

"How can that be," Tammy asked. "Are we not supposed to take pride in how we carry ourselves, act, or the things we accomplish in life?"

"Yes you must always carry yourself with pride, but you must never be prideful."

"I don't get it," Tammy responded. "Isn't that the same exact thing?"

"It is one thing to carry yourself with much pride and confidence, and it's another thing to be completely prideful. A person with pride will stand up for what they feel is right, while a prideful person will always feel that they are always right.

Like I've told you before, the moment you think you have the answers to all of life's questions and problems, you have failed yourself. Pride convinces you that you yourself are God. And what else can you teach an idiot who thinks they know everything? You have completely eliminated all of your future blessings by being prideful instead of humbling yourself to the possibility of what knowledge you're missing out on from others.

A person with pride works hard to rely only on themselves, but realizes that everything is possible through God. They know that it was Him who has surrounded you with the people you need to accomplish whatever task you need to when you don't have all of the tools. A prideful person is so busy knowing it all and therefore feels like they don't need anyone or anything but themselves to get where they want to go.

A person with pride understands that they are only human and are going to make mistakes. Hell, we were all born sinners, so we have to constantly ask the man upstairs for forgiveness. There is no problem in admitting that you've messed up and that you would like a second chance. A prideful person will flat-out refuse to apologize because they think they have all the answers once again.

Love is not prideful, and there are way too many complications in relationships to add too much damn pride in the mix! Love is about submitting to all of that pride by recognizing that all of that crap you're so busy harboring isn't going to keep you warm or company at night when that other person gets tired of your shit.

Life is all about choices, baby girl. You get to decide who you are and what part you play. What choice are you going to make?"

| 14 |

F*ck Men

"Fuck men and all of their bullshit," Tammy said as Tanya, Nina, and Tiffany held their shot glasses up with hers for a toast. "From now on, it's fuck niggas – let's get this money."

Tammy missed Patrick terribly, and even after her conversation with Ms. Cruz, her pride would not allow her to make the first move. It had been almost a week since she had seen or heard from him. She had been spending more time with her girls and alcohol and less time home alone, worrying about how much she missed just being around Patrick.

Jason had tried to comfort Tammy when he noticed Patrick leaving the building. He knew his friend was going to be upset when he found out the secret Tammy had been keeping, but he had no idea he was going to be so angry. His best friend walked right past him without acknowledging or speaking to him.

"Patrick is not like anyone you've met or dealt with before," Jason said as he came in and joined Tammy on the couch in the living room.

Tammy wasn't in the mood to talk to anyone, so she especially didn't want to talk to Jason of all people about her man issues. Jason had been trying hard to be nice and friendly with her ever since he dropped the news on her that day in Ms. Cruz's apartment. Realizing his genuine effort made it easier for Tammy to make the decision to soften up to him a little more.

"I know that I can be quite a bitch to you," Tammy started softly. "But I am just not ready to talk about it yet. I don't even think that when I'm finally ready to talk about it that I will be able to talk to you about it. How am I supposed to pour out my feelings to my father's employee and Patrick's best friend? How will I be able to truly trust that you won't spill everything to him now that the cat is out of the bag?"

He sat up from his comfortable position and turned in to face her. "Why are you so scared to let any man in to know you," Jason asked her. "I get that even though your dad is finally in your life, you guys don't have a normal relationship like most girls do with their fathers, but it's almost like you've shunned all men out too. Why? Don't you know you'll always have this kind of relationship with men unless you decide to do something different?

Unlike every other man in your life, I don't want anything from you. My life isn't going to change whether or not I have a single conversation with you. Who cares that Patrick has been my best friend almost all of my life? Didn't I hold the secret that you asked me to keep for you? I didn't have to do that shit. Truthfully, I could have been told your father where you've been and who you've been running around these streets with, but I never did that. I held it down for you, and now my boy isn't speaking to me, and my boss will probably have me killed if he finds out that I knew and never said anything about it to him."

Tammy had never looked at it that way before. *I guess he •oes have a point. This man coul• have tol• my father about this the moment he foun• out an• ha• all of our lives change• for it,* she thought to herself. At that moment, she decided that Jason deserved much more credit than she gave him.

"I thought I was protecting myself and my father by waiting to tell him," she said. "Having you follow me around all of those years while I was so oblivious just opened my eyes that I'm not as careful in this game as I need to be. I'm new to all of this street shit. I didn't have to grow up like this, and I never considered just how different life has to be for me because of it."

"I hear you, and I don't blame you for feeling the way that you do about everything. Patrick just needs some time to sort through this, and when he's not so mad, you should hit him up. Rick isn't going to fall into any of your traps like all the men before him, so I think you should know that before you go off trying to play with fire. Whatever games have worked on others will not work on him. He's not built like that. He's not trying to play any of those childish games."

Tammy heeded his advice, and despite the suggestion that Ms. Cruz had made, she thought some time and space may be good for them after all.

Since they had called things off, Tammy figured she didn't have to worry about Patrick or his friends showing up that night like they previously planned, but she was wrong.

She noticed him as soon as he walked in and flashed his signature smile at the hostess before she seated Patrick and his four friends at the table directly across from where Tammy and her friends were sitting.

Tammy sat in her seat nervously, but she tried her best to remain calm and relaxed. They briefly made eye contact as he took his seat, and just as she had expected, he didn't bother acknowledging her.

The rest of her meal was awkward. It was hard to sit there as she tried to forget that the man that had not left her mind since they met was so close to her physically, yet mentally way too far away. Despite all of the time they had spent together and the passion they shared, she wasn't going to play herself by trying to talk to him.

The girls had just finished another round of shots when Patrick got up and made his way to her table.

"Don't you have something to say to me," he said bluntly as he fixed his watch.

Tammy couldn't help but grin at his apparent attempt at making peace. Like her, Patrick carried himself with way too much pride to let this slide or be the one to make it right and apologize, but it was evident that he wanted things to be right between them. Tammy had played that trick way too many times to not realize when it was being done to her.

"Yeah," she replied timidly. "Why don't we go somewhere more private and discuss this?"

"For what," he asked. "If you mean what you're about to say, then you won't have any issues saying it in front of anyone and especially not your own friends,"

Tammy gave him a glare as if to plead with him. He knew that Tammy wanted to make things right but just had a problem saying what he wanted to hear in front of her friends. Even though he didn't want to play her in front of her girls, it was the only way he would know if she was serious about the feelings she said she actually had for him.

"Well," he said with a sly grin.

"I'm sorry, and you were right," Tammy replied back. "Are you happy now?"

The girls looked at Tammy in disbelief and back at Patrick in utter amazement. In all the years they had known Tammy, they knew it was way out of her character to apologize to anyone - especially a man.

"That wasn't so hard," he laughed as he extended his hand to grab hers.

In the excitement of having Patrick back without having to work as hard as she thought she was going to have to, she pulled out a hundred-dollar bill to cover their tab and dinner.

"I'll catch up with you bitches later," Tammy said with a smile as she grabbed his hand and slid out of the booth.

"So much for fuck men," Tanya yelled out to Tammy.

***

"Who was that hateful broad," Patrick asked once they were both comfortably in his car.

Tammy giggled. "That's just my girl, Tanya. She's always like that, but she's cool. She was the first person I met up here almost five years ago."

"Is that right? What makes her so cool anyway," he asked her with much curiosity.

"She was the first female I ever met that was ready to bang for me when shit got real. No one before her ever bothered to do that for me," Tammy responded.

"Look at Beast. That nigga has always been a hit first ask questions later type of guy, so that doesn't mean shit," he replied flatly. "Some broads just like to fight, and that ghetto bird looks like she is one of them."

Tammy was taken back at his obvious jab at Tanya. He didn't even say one word to her for him to be making any kind of assumptions about her. She really found it strange that they had a conversation about the importance of not judging others just a few months ago. Now, he suddenly had so much to say.

One night during their getaway, they stopped inside of a local gas station for some snacks before they returned back to their suite to call it a night. Just as they were leaving the store, they noticed a man standing outside begging for change.

Patrick watched Tammy walk right by the man ignoring his pleas for something to eat before she got into his car.

She sat there as she watched Patrick chat for a moment with the old homeless man.

Damn he always knows someone everywhere we freaking go, she thought to herself.

Once he was finished speaking with the man, she noticed him pull out a couple dollars and a few snacks and handed them to the man before he dapped him up and made his way to the car.

"Well, that was very sweet of you. Who know you had such a soft spot?" Tammy stated once he sat down.

"Well, I had to make up for your rudeness after all," Patrick responded bluntly.

"I'm not giving my hard-earned money to some bum-ass drug addict. I have to work hard for every dollar I get, and so should he. We all have the same opportunities. No one told that nigga to make poor choices with his life. Why the hell should I have to pay for it," she spoke up, not even bothering to hide the disgust in her voice.

"It's so ugly how judgmental you are," he responded as he pulled the car away from the store to head back to the hotel. "Have you ever been homeless before?"

"No," she responded.

"Then you should thank God. It's not easy relying on the kindness of others just to survive. Trust me, I know about it personally, and I'm no drug addict.

Your job is not to judge anyone because your hands are not clean enough to be throwing any kinds of stones," Patrick stated.

Remembering just how he tried to school her that day for judging someone she didn't know, she was eager to get to the bottom of his accusations about Tanya.

"How can you sit up here and judge my homegirl when your friends do what they do," she asked him.

"I'm not going to go into what those in my circle got going on, but I can tell you that I wouldn't have survived in these streets as long as I have if I wasn't good at reading people or trusting my intuition. Something is just not right about that girl, and I can tell."

***

Once Tammy and Patrick made up, they couldn't keep their hands off of each other. They got another suite and enjoyed each other's company for a full two weeks.

"Well, well, well, how nice of you to remember where you live," Jason said as he opened the door to let Tammy in. "Your pops is finally starting to get really suspicious of all of this time you've spent away from the house that has been unaccounted for."

Tammy's eyes got wide in surprise. Delino typically stayed out of her personal business. However, she was still nervous to find out how her father would react to the man she chose to settle down with.

"What did you tell him," she asked fretfully.

"I ain't say shit. He knows I've been on my job with keeping you safe, and that's all I care about. I don't want him to know I knew shit about what you two have going on. Oh," he said as he made his way to the living room. "Derrick keeps dropping shit off for you. Your room is filled with all types of crap. I told you that you need to dead that nigga because he is going to be a problem."

"Aw," Tammy said as she joined him on the couch. "That's cute that you're looking out for your friend, but I can assure you he has nothing to worry about with other men, especially not Derrick of all people."

"Tammy, please," he said with a chuckle. "You really think my boy would be worried about any of his runners like that? All he wants from them niggas is sealed lips and all of his money. I'm telling you to watch out for him because something just doesn't feel right with how he has been carrying on lately. I think you really drove that man crazy. There is something really unsettling about dealing with a desperate ass nigga, and you don't want to find out how ugly that can get."

"What's up with you and Patrick being all up in your feelings and shit," she asked.

"No one is in their feelings," he said, correcting her. "I just really learned how to trust my instincts. That little voice that tells you something isn't right, you really have to learn to trust it. Patrick and I have avoided a lot of trouble that way. We've also scored some big licks all off of our gut feelings."

"What the hell does that mean," Tammy asked. "What the hell is a lick anyway?"

"Damn," Jason whispered. "I guess you guys haven't dug that deep in your pasts just yet. You're just going to have to let him get into all of that with you."

***

"Hmm," Tanya said with an ugly glare as Tammy sat down to join her for lunch. "You love pulling this disappearing act on me so often now. I never know when you'll just go ghost on a bitch anymore."

"Relax, Tanya. Your time is going to come, boo. One day you'll find love and know exactly why I am acting the way that I have been lately," Tammy declared with a smile.

"I would pump my brakes if I were you talking about all of that love shit because there is a lot of things you don't know about your so called lover boy."

"Well obviously," Tammy said, not removing her eyes from the menu she was grazing over. "There is also a lot I don't know about you, but you don't see me giving you shit every damn day."

"You are about to be under a lot of stress, so I'm going to let that foolishness slide," Tanya said in a matter-of-fact tone.

"Excuse you," Tammy responded as she finally laid her menu down and leaned in closer to the table. "Was that supposed to be a threat or something?"

"Bitch please," Tanya said as she rolled her eyes. "If I was going to fuck you up, I wouldn't warn you.

I'm actually trying to help your unappreciative ass out if you would shut up and listen. Get this, I was super curious about your boy, and after you left, I did a little digging around on him for you. Don't worry," she said, waving her hand. "You can thank me later. Anyway, that woman by the bar in the red dress can tell you everything you need to know about this nigga that has you acting funny."

Tammy typically didn't listen to he-said-she-said, but the advice was coming through Tanya, and the fact that she seemed to find out one of his secrets every day left her more curious about the man she gave her heart to.

***

After Tammy and Jason had finished up their conversation, she immediately reached out to Patrick to see what other skeletons he had been keeping from her.

"What the hell is a lick, and how long have you been doing it," she asked bluntly.

Patrick's sweet tone that he had answered the phone with completely went cold as he pressed his lips to the phone and sternly spoke. "How dare you talk to me like this over the fucking phone? I'm coming to deal with you right now."

Thirty minutes later, there was a light knock at her door, and she knew by the rhythm of the knocks that it was Patrick on the other end.

Jason went to open the door for his friend, and he decided to give the two of them some privacy as they had time to discuss the question that Tammy had originally called to ask him.

"It's crazy how I seem to learn something new about you every damn day," Tammy stated once the door was closed.

"Are you seriously acting like this because of a few things that I've done in my past?"

"Yes, I am," Tammy yelled. "I called around to get the answer to my question, so I already know what you're about to admit to. On top of everything that you already are, you are also a fucking thief," she said.

"Let's get one thing absolutely clear here," he started. "I am no fucking thief. I am simply an opportunist."

"Of course, I should leave it to the smooth talker to find a clever way to get around admitting what he actually is," Tammy stated sarcastically. "You take things that don't belong to you, so to put it frankly - you steal. If you steal, that makes you a thief. Obviously, you struggled with definitions in school, so I figured I would help clear it up for you."

"Do you not understand that most people don't have the same opportunities that you've had growing up? You can sit here and paint up your sad stories however you want to for whoever you want to, but you have no idea about where I even come from.

I had to move away from Boston, Massachusetts because I've made way too many enemies over there. Of course, they share that same small-minded mentality that you do and just see me like some fucking thief, but that's not it at all.

My parents moved us up here from Jamaica to show us the fucking American dream. Little did they know, the dream was free to have but to actually obtain it would require a lot of damn work. I never did anything that I didn't feel was necessary for survival. I'm not one of these greedy niggas you see out here that just takes just to do it.

I learned to use the fact that I could smooth-talk anyone to my advantage. If you had something I needed, then I was going to get it however I needed to. When I didn't have the money to buy product, I did whatever I needed to in order to get it. I just kept doing my thing until I was finally in a position that I could actually help other people around me.

You think I enjoy living this life," he asked her as he changed the direction of the conversation. "I'm way too old now to be living my life like this still. I never thought I would be doing this shit at my age, but I'm at a point that I have no other choice. I'm a convicted felon over some bullshit mistakes that I made as a young kid. I can't get a regular nine to five that will pay me enough to live like I do and help support those in my circle, so I put my life on the line to make sure that everyone around me is good. Do you really think that makes me a bad person?"

Tammy never responded because, for once, she felt like she was on the opposite end of all of the bullshit she had been given by her own family. She knew what it felt like to want to create a better life for other people, even if it wasn't done conventionally. Truthfully, she finally met someone that she thought she understood his reasons for doing the things he did.

"No, I guess it doesn't make you a bad person," she responded. "Does it make me a bad person for finding you even more attractive after understanding you more," she giggled.

"You like to say you love me," he said as he moved in closer to her on the couch and put his arm around her, "But it's obvious that you really don't because if you did, I wouldn't go through this with you every week."

"It's because I actually do that I act this way with you," Tammy responded in a matter-of-fact tone. "It's weird. I'm just not used to caring about someone the way I do with you."

"Well, then why does it seem like you fight your feelings and find reasons not to deal with me instead of embracing who and what I am? It sounds to me like you're just afraid to really love me."

"I'm not afraid to love you," she spoke up timidly. "I'm just afraid of what loving you can do to me. I've never cared about another human the way that I do for you. I've never connected or wanted to be close to anyone else like I want to with you. This is all so new to me. I'm not really an emotional person, and you seem to bring out just about every kind of emotion out of me. I don't know how to handle it sometimes. In an effort to not feel so crazy for dealing with you, I actually started writing again. I hadn't written a poem for almost 8 years, and then I start dealing with you, and now I just can't seem to stop writing them."

"I've heard about these so-called skills you have, but I have yet to actually hear something from you," Patrick responded.

Tammy got up from her spot on the couch and went to her room to retrieve a yellow and pink notebook. Patrick recognized the notebook because just a few weeks into meeting her, she bought it and began taking it with her everywhere she went.

"This is the first poem I wrote in almost a decade," Tammy said as she sat in close to him. "Please, keep all of your smart-ass comments to yourself because I'm super sensitive about my shit," she stated seriously.

He shrugged his shoulders and gave her a grin as he watched Tammy nervously recite her poem.

"Your subtle kisses are the sweetest things I've ever felt;

Yet your love is venomous for me.

I want to forget you but you're a part of this hand I was dealt

So I try but I can't find a way to just let you be

One glance into your brown eyes and I seem to lose all of my common sense.

The window to your soul sucks me in and keeps me confined

No matter how hard I contest—I'm weak and sadly so is all of my defense

It's frightening to me because this is not how I was designed.

"Guard your heart," my mother constantly said. "Don't ever let a man in."

I take heed to her words because she's always seemed to be right,

But no matter the size of the battle you always seem to win.

Because once you smile that enchanting smile I lose all of my will to fight.

I can finally admit defeat – This superwoman has finally found her kryptonite."

Once Tammy had finished her poem, Patrick leaned in and kissed her gently on her forehead.

"You're so confident to be so shy about the best part of you," he declared. "That was good. You need to stop keeping all of that talent just bottled in to yourself."

Tammy blushed. "Do you really like it or are you just trying to make me feel good about myself."

"Nah, I really think you could be the next Edgar Allan Poe," he responded.

"Damn. Thanks. No one has ever compared my poems to one of a literary beast."

"Truthfully, sweetie, I didn't mean it as a direct compliment. Listen, not everyone is able to do what you do by putting feelings down on paper in such a nice way. You manage to hide behind this tough exterior when you have such beautiful poetry inside of you. If you continue this way, like Edgar Allan Poe, niggas won't find out about how talented you are until it's too late."

***

After their conversation and her getting a better understanding of Patrick, they seemed to be right back in their honeymoon phase again. Tammy almost didn't want it to be over by finding out any more of his secrets.

"The woman at the bar's name is Josie," Tanya said when she noticed the hesitant Tammy hadn't left the table yet. "She's the mother of his kids and his live-in wife."

Tammy had always wondered why he never took her to his own house but never made a big enough deal to press it. Instead, she realized that he was probably just as careful as she was about the location of where he and his children would lay their heads on night. He had been honest to her from the very beginning that he had children, and Tammy didn't have a problem with that. In fact, Tammy loved children and loved the possibility of one day meeting his kids. However, he never divulged into any conversations about any other woman or the possibility that he was still together with his children's mother.

Reluctantly, Tammy got up from her seat at the table and sat next to the woman at the bar.

"So you're the whore that's been keeping him away from his family," she said flatly, never removing her eyes from the cosmopolitan she had been drinking.

"Excuse me," Tammy asked, clearly confused.

"Bitch you heard me," the woman said, turning her attention to Tammy finally. "I'm sick of little birds like you who think that you're actually going to take my place or my fucking family."

Tammy was not much of a confrontational person. She knew that with the flood of emotions that had her floored, she would end up killing the woman if she allowed the anger she was feeling to rear its ugly head. Instead of letting this woman to see her weakness as the emotions took control, she got up and left the restaurant without saying another word to the woman or to Tanya.

Once she was outside, she allowed the tears she had been holding in to fall freely since the soft raindrops falling on her helped to mask the pain to those walking by.

"You better leave him alone," she heard the woman call out to her, "Or I'm going to *kill* you myself."

| 15 |

A Hood Love Story

"Why can't I stop crying," Tammy asked as Ms. Cruz gently rubbed her back. "It's been two weeks, and I haven't seen him or answered any of his calls, and I still can't forget him, her, or the memories that I had with him. Why does this actually hurt so much?"

"Mi amor," Ms. Cruz stated softly as she sat Tammy up from her comfortable spot she had been laying in with her head in her lap. She looked her in her eyes and continued.

"I wish I could answer that for you or tell you what you needed to hear to help bring you comfort, but only one knows exactly why you are going through this right now. Only He knows everything. We can't only enjoy the sunshine and the happiness that life and love bring. We also need to trust the pain and disappointment that comes with the hurt and the rain too.

Every person in your life that you encounter has a purpose. Some will love you, some will hurt you, and others are there to push you. Either way, all of their roles are important, and you'll thank them all as you grow into the woman you are supposed to be because of them.

I think now is as good as ever to finally tell you more about my sweet Lorenzo, that is if you're up to hear about it right now?"

Tammy was heartbroken, but she had waited anxiously for the details of their love story. She nodded in excitement.

"The reason Lorenzo and I really worked together is because we trusted each other fully; we never had to prove anything to each other. He understood the power and hold he had on me, and I trusted him never to abuse it. I'm sure it was the same for him since he told me things that I know he had never shared with another human. Because of this, I let him be who he was, and he let me just be me. What your generation seems to be confused about is that love is not about ownership. It's about being so selfless that you put their happiness above yours. You have to allow them to be free to do whatever they want, but leave them with enough to have a reason to come back. Love is about seeing someone full of flaws flawlessly. It's about seeing the darkest and dustiest part of someone and riding it through with them anyway.

Lorenzo loved women, and I knew that from the moment I laid eyes on him that he was the kind of man that women threw themselves all over. He was charming, and that presence he had just demanded your attention and respect. It's no wonder that his ex-wife and I had a similar showdown when I met her. Some women truly believe that having a baby with a man gives her ownership or some kind of power over him. Still, men like Lorenzo, Lino, and Patrick are not meant to be contained or confined.

Anyway, I was angry with him for not being honest about her role in his life. He then explained that she was the mother of his children and that her role was permanent, but not the role she was hoping for. She really thought that scaring every woman off that tried to love him would mean that he would have no choice but to come back and be with her. But when love is real, there is nothing anyone can say or do to keep two people apart that the Lord has put together for a purpose.

Truthfully, I don't know the situation between him and this woman. I've never met or heard of her. I can only give you the advice that I wish someone would have given to me so that I didn't have to spend so much time fighting my feelings and emotions for the only man I had ever loved or given myself to. I would have done it more freely if I had realized that the time I had with him wasn't forever like we planned. I wouldn't have been afraid to sit down and have the hard decisions the moment I could if I would have known that years without him would feel like an eternity. Unlike what romance novels will have you to believe, real relationships require real work," Ms. Cruz continued.

"Just remember, there is potential for everyone in this world. You and Patrick have the possibility to be the fairy tale book happy ever after that so many people spend their lives searching for. Still, there is an equal percentage that he will just be a villain you one day write about. When you think with your heart, make sure that you're actually in love with that person for who they are and not for who you think you can turn them into or what you want them to be.

Maybe after all of this love you've finally given to him and the trust that you've shown him, he's already fulfilled his purpose in your life. He turned that small flame that we are all born with and sparked it into a massive fire. For once, you felt like you could just be free. I get it because Lorenzo was that man for me. I will forever cherish the time that I spent sharing my life with him because it was a great experience. The good times and the bad ones turned me into the woman I needed to be. I accepted his flaws and his strengths and everything else in between, and when it was time to let it go, I did just that," Ms. Cruz declared.

"If you two truly loved each other and accepted each other, then why did you two have to say goodbye," Tammy asked as she dried the tears from her eyes. "If the love you two had was so real, then why isn't he here today?"

"I'm going to tell you, but I don't think you'll actually believe me," she chuckled. "Sometimes, it's hard to believe the story myself when I sit down and think of it.

Anyway, he and I were a deadly team. Because we trusted each other so much, we put ourselves in some very compromising situations. He was a pilot with his planes and fancy homes, so he had many ways to easily transport large amounts of product. I was the beauty and the brains. I used my gift of manipulation and sexiness to increase our business.

We stole, lied, we fled, we loved, and that's all we were put together to do. We made a lot of money together and committed a lot of crimes doing it, and I'm sure your mother taught you that what happens in the dark eventually is going to come to light.

The feds eventually caught up to us. Well, him, actually. Because I had allowed him to do what he wanted, he kept other beautiful women around that helped us complete our crimes along the way. To the feds, I was just as disposable as the rest of them, and I allowed them to think that because it was the best thing for both of us." Ms. Cruz's voice started to crack as it became evident that reliving that moment was very painful.

"He gave me the option to spend my life fleeing with him. It would have given us a chance to see different countries, places, and cultures, which is something we both passionately wanted to do. Still, I knew we couldn't live like that forever. He had a little spot that he could visit and lay low for a while, and I told him to go there. It would be easier for the feds to one day find us if we ran together because we would be committing crimes all the way through in order to survive.

I loved that man so much that I gave up the chance to enjoy forever to make sure that he could live his life peacefully. He had worked so hard for so long that he really deserved that. I had a small funeral for his death," she said with a wink. "So I could say my final goodbyes to the love of my life. The feds' investigation was forced to be closed with no other leads, and I'll live forever with the joys of knowing him and loving him left me with," she said as a small tear escaped.

"Anyway," she continued. "He was my mirror. I loved him because I was able to see myself in him. Everything I had tried so hard to avoid, he showed me that it was ok to just be me and to be true to who I was regardless of what others thought," Ms. Cruz continued.

"We are drawn to people similar to us but rarely do you meet someone and fully relate to them, their story, and their soul. When you do, you're supposed to cherish those people – not judge them like everyone else does.

Take it from an old woman who has literally been there done that and has lived more lives in 10 years than some do in their entire life. Too much of our lives are spent just merely existing. Too much of our lives are simply mediocre. We work mediocre jobs, for barely mediocre paychecks that provide less than mediocre lives. If there is one part of your life that shouldn't be mediocre, it's your love life. If your love is not passionate – it's just not fucking worth it."

***

Like always, Ms. Cruz's advice left Tammy more confused than before. Ms. Cruz was always careful to never provide her own thoughts and feelings of what someone else should do because she was always preaching the importance of doing the right thing.

After hiding out and moping around Ms. Cruz's apartment for two weeks, Tammy finally thought it was time to go home. To her surprise, this time, it was her father that answered the door.

"Well, well, well, look what the cat finally brought home," he said as he held the door and blocked the entrance for Tammy to enter the apartment.

Tammy wasn't in the mood to argue, and she definitely didn't want to have to tell her dad what was going on in her life.

"Hey," she stated timidly as she tried to make her way inside.

"That's not going to work this time," he said. "I'm actually taking time off to figure out what the hell is going on with you, so what's up," he asked, still not moving out of the way.

"Can I just have a chance to get in and settle down before we talk," she asked slightly irritably.

"Hmm," he said as he moved from in front of the door to let her in.

As soon as Tammy was in the apartment, she noticed Jason in the living room as she made her way to her bedroom. She really didn't want to deal with her father and Jason in the same night, especially because she had been avoiding Patrick's call.

"So which one of you is finally going to have the balls to tell me what is going on?" Delino asked as he took his seat in his comfortable leather lazy boy recliner.

"I'm not going into my personal life with one of your employees present," Tammy said flatly.

"Cut the crap, Tee. I already know that you know Jason and the fact that he has been following you. Again, which one of you is going to tell me what's going on," he asked again.

Regardless of what was going on, Tammy started to look at Jason as one of her friends and didn't want to see him get in trouble.

"I really don't know what you're talking about. I don't associate with the help," Tammy said with an attitude. "If you want to actually sit down and have a father and daughter conversation with me, then let's do it the right way and have it one-on-one. If that's too much to ask for from you, then I will be in my room," Tammy said as she made her way to her bedroom.

Delino didn't press the issue any further. Since he and Tammy had started working on a relationship, Tammy had lost her nasty attitude with him for the most part.

"Be ready in an hour. We are going out to eat," Delino demanded before she closed the door to her bedroom to sulk in what had become her life.

Tammy wasn't really in the mood to spend time with her father, but she realized that he rarely took time off work. The fact that he was willing to go out to eat, something he rarely did, showed that he was really concerned.

They arrived at the restaurant, and the owner came out to greet Lino personally. They were led to the back to a quiet and secluded area, just like Lino preferred when he finally decided to switch up his schedule and eat out.

"So what's going on, Tee? I know that you're grown and can move around like you want to. But you've been moving a little funny lately. You've been spending so much time away from the house and giving my man Jason a hard time with keeping tabs on you. What are you trying to hide from me," he asked with genuine concern.

"Do you really think I'm dumb," Tammy asked him. "I saw him following me months ago and decided to throw him off. I don't like feeling like I have eyes on me all the time like I'm some kind of baby or something."

"I run these streets, Tee. Even when I don't say anything, I know exactly what's going on. Stop trying to cover for your new friend and just tell me the truth."

Tammy wasn't sure if her father was calling her bluff or not, so she really didn't want to do anything that could get Jason in trouble.

"I really don't know-," Tammy started before her father cut her off.

"You're seeing Patrick Bennett, who happens to be a good friend of the employee that I trusted with your life. Does that sound familiar at all," he asked her. "I truly commend your loyalty, and it's things like that that really remind me that you are my daughter," he said with a chuckle. "Don't worry, he is not going to be in any kind of trouble. I can see that means a lot to you, even though the father part of me wants to have him dismembered tonight," Lino tittered.

Lino's last statement immediately brought goosebumps to Tammy's skin. Although she had never seen her father in action, she knew that her father wasn't a man to play with.

"Please just tell me what is going on with you," he continued. "You have been distant. You stopped coming home and enjoying dinner with me like we used to do. Believe it or not, I miss those times – even though sometimes they were spent in complete silence. To me, it was just nice to see you smile or have you around. Now, whenever I do see you, it just seems like you're sad or unhappy. What's going on?"

She was actually quite relieved that he knew and seemed to be okay with it.

"I don't know, dad," she started. "For the first time in my life, I decided to love the idea of love, and that bitch just didn't love me back," Tammy stated before a small tear formed in the corner of her eye.

Like Mariana, Delino was not an emotional man and couldn't handle the idea of seeing his daughter cry.

"Please don't start that shit," he said bluntly. "I know your mother raised you to be stronger than that. Crying doesn't do shit but tire you out and give you a headache. Tell me exactly what happened and save the waterworks." He took a deep breath to compose himself. "I didn't mean that to come off as harsh as it did. All I'm trying to say is that crying has never solved a single problem. I guess that's why I haven't done it since I was five. Honestly, it's just hard for me to be sympathetic for others when it seems no one has ever been that way for me. If you need to cry, then cry. Please just don't expect me to be able to console you the way you probably need, though."

Before Tammy started her story, she made her father swear to secrecy. She did her best to tell her father what was wrong with her but left out details that she knew would upset him.

"So you think he was possibly seeing another woman, and that's what you're sitting up here getting all emotional over," he asked. "The only one that will be able to answer that question is Patrick himself, and it sounds to me like you're denying him the chance to tell his side of the story. But I can tell you now that you will stress yourself out if you live your life worrying about what other people are doing. You will always be a prisoner to your mind and emotions until you realize that people will do whatever they want to do regardless of how the hell you feel.

Anyway, everyone has a different perception of what cheating is," he said as he took a sip of his Heineken. "Show me a man who said he doesn't cheat or never cheated, and I'll easily show you a fucking liar."

"Why do you have to think so negatively all the time," Tammy asked. "Don't you think that there are actually men out there that are capable of being just as loyal and loving as women are?"

"It's not that I don't think that people are not capable of doing right by you. I just believe that you're really an idiot if you think you can know the thoughts of another man. Don't ever put your trust and expectations on people, not even me or your mother, because we are only human, and we will let you down. At the end, no matter what, do not trust any fucking body. Trust yourself and God – that's it. Those are the only two people you can truly depend on. And if you are someone who is really honest with yourself, then you'll realize that sometimes you can't even trust yourself. Because when time and opportunity align at the perfect intersection, we are all capable of doing things we thought we would never do.

Everyone is the star of their own reality world," He continued. "Don't base your story on what role you want someone to play in it because you're only going to end up hurting yourself. As much as we like to convince ourselves of the power we have, no one has the power to control the heart or motives of someone else.

Delino took a deep sigh before he continued.

"Then, to make matters worse, you would choose a man like me, and he's so much older than you. That's something I never wanted for you," Delino sighed again. "I know what kind of lifestyle a man like that can give you, and I can tell you that you deserve better than that. Look at you. You're so smart. You're about to be 21, and you already have your own business and cosmetic line. How many girls your age can honestly say that they will achieve that in their life, much less at such a young age?

I'm not going to tell you what to do because I know you are just going to do the exact opposite," he chuckled. "I just can't wait to see you back in school and being the woman I know you can be. You're better than this, and you're better than to deal with someone so similar to me. You're a sweetheart, and you deserve a sweet man or at least one of those square men you see on the TV shows. You deserve someone who will sweep you off of your feet and cater to your every need. You deserve a man who will be man enough to do what makes you happy each and every day and someone who is going to remind you of how beautiful you are all the time. Find a man like that. Maybe because of the choices that I've made in life, I've never met someone up close like that. But if there is anyone in the world that can find that person, I believe you could," Delino stated sincerely.

"What if that's not what I want," Tammy asked. "I just want to be me, and anyone who wants to deal with that is going to have to understand that. I'm not some push-over woman who can handle a man who has no balls. For crying out loud, the only guy I really opened up to was Patrick, and you are not a soft man yourself. Do you really think I could handle being with someone like that?"

"It took you almost a year to decide on the name of your cosmetic line," Delino pointed out. "Once you finally figured it out, you were so indecisive on what products and colors you were going to have. You don't even know what you want for this business that you've been talking about for years. How do you really know at 21 what kind of man you're going to need for the rest of your life? How do you really know you don't like something if you never really opened yourself up to truly trying it? You're just as much of a sweetheart as you are a hard-headed asshole. It's just been easier to be the bitch, but that's only because that's what you're comfortable doing.

I'm going to be honest with you," he said as he took another sip to clear his throat. "Men like Patrick and I don't change. We've spent so many years changing the way our minds think, so we don't think with our hearts. If it doesn't sound like a logical soundproof plan in our mind, or if it doesn't make any money, then it's not worth it to us. In this game, you always have to ask yourself, 'How much are you willing to risk if what you lost you had to charge it to the game?' Every day Patrick and I take losses. If it's not a loss of money or product, we are losing a runner or an officer off our payroll. We charge a lot of shit to this game every single day, and one thing we aren't willing to wager with is our hearts.

Look at me," he paused for a moment before he continued. "I loved your mother with all of my heart. I never loved like that before her or after her because I knew that no one would be able to replace her. She was the woman that was meant for me and I let her go because of my pride and because of this game I play. Even now, I know that is really how I feel, but if she were here, I would deny it with everything in me. My pride won't allow me to show someone just how much they can or have hurt me.

I had so much money and women at one time in my life, both objects were disposable to me. Your mom, though, she took a lot of shit from me. I knew I would never find another woman who would ride for me and remain as loyal to me as your mother had been for me all of those years. I can find a beautiful woman, a sexy one, a freaky one,

one to cook, one to clean, one to cater to my needs, but no amount of money can make a woman loyal to you.

I always thought she would never leave me. Because of you and your brother and all of the years we had spent together, I thought I didn't have to do anything to get her to stay. I thought once I had put her back in a colossal condo or house, she would have been happy, and everything would have gone back to normal, but even though I loved her, I was not what she needed.

He told her things I never told her because I was too busy out here in these streets. He didn't have the money that I had to buy her the gifts I showered her with, but he had the time to show her how valuable she actually was. He took the time to invest in the future and lives of two children he didn't father and made my life much easier in the process.

I never wanted to not be a part of your lives. Believe it or not, every birthday or holiday that passed really bothered me to know that you guys were one happy family instead of with me where you guys always belonged. I knew that if I would have gone into early retirement or slowed down in these streets, I could have come to get you guys and had my family back where I wanted you guys, but I knew that would be selfish of me.

Richard was the kind of man emotionally that you guys needed. Even though he couldn't do what I could do for you financially, the time he was able to give you guys was worth way more than any money I could have given you guys."

Delino had never opened up to her like this before. Tammy almost didn't know how to respond to her father since this was so outside of his character. Instead of speaking up, she waited silently to see if he would continue. After a few minutes of silence, he did.

"I don't need you to tell me that your mom was a complete bitch to Richard," Delino said with an awkward chuckle. "I had left that woman broken and with so many scars, so I know she felt like she needed to protect herself from anyone she dealt with after me. Promise me that you won't do that.

Growing up, my father used to tell me the one clue to know when you have found the right woman is in how she talks to you. He would remind me that every man has two men inside of him, an idiot and a king. Your mother always talked to the king in me. Well, except for when she was pissed off," he stated with a snicker. "I loved that about her. She was a woman with class, and she respected her body which forced me to respect it too.

She was hard-working, business-oriented, and when I first met her, she talked to the hustler in me and not like some goal digger just looking for a quick come-up.

What I'm telling you may not make sense now, but when you find the right one, everything I'm saying is going to click for you. You are going to get this advice the moment you are supposed to and not a moment sooner."

Again, Delino paused and deeply sighed before he continued.

"I'm your father, and even though I've never told you this, I want you to know that I love you more than anything. I only want the best for you, and I'm going to be here for you always, no matter what. Nothing is going to keep your old man away from you ever again."

| 16 |

Tomorrow

"I've never done this before," Tammy spoke softly into the microphone. "Keep all of your negative comments and smirks to yourself because I'm serious about this stuff. I'm only doing this for him."

She unfolded the paper she previously had in her purse. She was afraid to speak, and then a sense of calmness washed over her as she had remembered some advice Patrick had given to her the very first time she read one of her poems out loud. Thanks to that, when she spoke into the microphone again, she did it with undeniable confidence and poise.

"The thing about tomorrow is that it's promised to no one yet we make plans with it anyway.

I'll do it tomorrow.

I'll call him tomorrow.

I'll be there tomorrow.

That's just a few of the things we say to push off something that actually needs to be done today.

If I would have known that the promises my father made to me that night would have never seen tomorrow I would have held on to each syllable a little tighter.

I would have cherished each hour, minute, and second I had of his most precious possession – his time.

I would have actually held him that night and I never would have let him go. Because for him, there would be no tomorrow.

The only thing tomorrow found was a fatherless girl,

Confused and angry at the whole wide world.

He never saw tomorrow,

And although I did, mine was filled with nothing but sorrow.

The problem is too many of us have gotten comfortable with the idea of tomorrow not realizing that today could be our last day to make amends and do what's right.

Today could be that last chance to hug a loved one or to let them know that they are cared for.

Today could be the last day to finish that daunting chore,

Or explore all of the things you've been searching for.

So do it today, and don't be like me and wait for tomorrow.

Because my tomorrows will be filled with the memories of the things I should have done when I had the chance to do it.

My tomorrows will contain the pain of the words I swallowed that night depending on a fucking tomorrow that never came.

My tomorrows will be filled with self-blame

As I drive myself insane

In a sea of words that I never got to explain

Because I was too busy waiting on tomorrow."

Tammy paused for a moment while she fought back the tears she had been holding on to for days. "I love you too daddy," she said as she got down from the podium and laid one hand on the casket where her father was resting peacefully.

***

Tammy never would have imagined that so many people would have shown up to her father's funeral. In all of the time she had been living with him, she had never paid much attention to how many people her father touched or had come in contact with on a daily basis. Her father's service lasted for hours as so many people came to the podium to share heart-wrenching stories of a man who considered himself "The heartless lion."

Tammy was glad that her father had actually opened up to her the way he did because Tammy was finally able to accept and appreciate the love that Richard gave to her when she needed him the most. Once Jason broke the news to Tammy that her father was gunned down shortly after he left the restaurant, she had a gut feeling to call Richard. She knew he would provide the love that she needed at that exact moment. Despite the ugliness and ungratefulness she had shown the man for many years, he never allowed that to stop the comfort he tried to cover her with.

Tammy was exhausted from the hours of planning the funeral, the actual service, and all of the time she spent meeting almost everyone her father knew and worked with. Jason had super tight security lined up with all of Delino's most trusted employees because even after almost a week, no one knew what had happened or who had shot him.

"Everyone is finally clearing out, and everything is moving smoothly. Your limo is in back waiting for you, so just let me know what you're ready to leave," Jason said to Tammy.

"Thanks, Jason," she spoke up. "I really appreciate you and everything that you've done for my father and me. I don't know where I'm going to be without you," Tammy stated meaning every word.

"What is that supposed to mean," he asked, confused. "I'm not going anywhere. Now that your father is out of the game, the streets are about to go crazy as everyone tries to take a spot at his throne. Now is the time to beef up security for you even more."

With the way that her father lived, Tammy never would had imagined that her father was worth the kind of money that she had heard so many people whispering about during the service.

"You're officially the boss now, kid," Jason responded. "There are things in place to make sure that you live just as good as your father did, so that means you're stuck with me."

She was already overwhelmed with everything that had occurred in such a short amount of time. In the course of a few weeks, Tammy had managed to lose the love of her life and her father while gaining all of her father's assets, businesses, and enemies.

"Jason, I'm ready to leave," the now light-headed Tammy said as she reached for his hand.

Jason walked with her hand in hand to the limo to make sure that she got there safely. As she was walking to the car, she noticed the man she had been avoiding for weeks standing just a few feet away from the limo.

"I'm so sorry about your loss," Patrick said sincerely as Tammy made her way into her seat. "I loved your father like he was my own. If there is anything I can do to help you out, please let me know. I promise you I won't rest until I found out exactly who did this and why," he declared.

"If I need you, I will be in touch. Until then, please stop calling me," Tammy said before she had Jason slammed the door.

| 17 |

Can You Handle It?

THREE YEARS LATER

"I honestly feel like the luckiest man in the world," Brian said to Tammy over dinner. "You've really made a name for yourself out here in Boston for being the best of the best businesswoman out here to work with, and you've shown that in the last few years I've been dealing with you. I'm just shocked you finally agreed to let me court you after chasing you around for so long."

"Well," Tammy said as she took a sip of her long Island Iced Tea. "You do realize that flattery gets you everywhere with me," she responded with a giggle. "I won't lie, at first I was very timid to do any kind of business with you because I thought you were hard-headed and stubborn. But you've proven yourself to be the exact opposite."

After her father's death, Tammy would become overwhelmed with emotions any time she was stuck inside any of the homes he owned in New York. Mariana, Tammy's mother, had begged her to move back home several times, but Tammy was not ready for the slow-paced lifestyle that living back in Orlando, Florida offered. Jason had suggested that she make a trip back home to Boston, Massachusetts. Once Tammy stayed in the condo her father had, she decided that she wanted to enjoy the city life a little longer.

She completed her father's wishes and enrolled back in school to major in business. Tammy was determined to fulfill her father's wishes before he was murdered.

"Well I'm glad you can finally see that," Brian said. "All of these gifts were beginning to add up, and you're not a cheap woman to shop for," he laughed. "I love a woman that knows what she wants, and that is definitely you."

Brian was far from Tammy's type. He was only 5'9 and had more on him to love than Tammy was used to. No matter what, though he loved to make money. More importantly, he loved to spend money on Tammy.

"I've already got the contracts written up to get your cosmetic line in almost every major boutique in the state of Massachusetts. The only thing I'm waiting on is your John Hancock. Do you have any idea how good it's going to feel once you are able to sign a 2.5 million dollar check with your name on it?"

The thought of making that kind of money instantly turned Tammy on, and she began to lose interest with the entire evening that they had planned out already.

"Fuck this night," Tammy said seductively. "Take me home right now."

"But the night is so early, and I really wanted to spend time with you," he tried to reason with her.

"Brian," Tammy snapped. "Shut the fuck up and take me back to your fucking house. Do I have to spell everything out for you," she asked irritably. "I try to talk to you with more respect and appreciate you for the king that you are, but my God, when will you learn to read between the lines."

Unable to contain his excitement, he pulled out his wallet and took two hundred dollar bills out to cover their drinks, appetizers, and the tip for the evening.

"I'm going to go to the lady's room to freshen up real quick," Tammy said as she got up from the table. "Make sure the car is ready for me when I get outside."

'Yes, ma'am," Brian said eagerly.

Tammy washed her hands and tried to kill a little time as she tried to get her thoughts together about what she was about to do.

Even though I always hated listening to you, you always seem to have all the right answers and suggestions old man. I'm going through with this, she thought as she removed the gold flask out of her clutch bag and allowed the Remy to warm her insides.

"*Please watch over me, Daddy,*" she prayed before she exited the building to see that Brian had done exactly what she had instructed him to do and had his Ferrari waiting on her.

They reached his home in Beacon Hill; Tammy immediately made herself at home.

"This is nice," she stated as she admired all of the fine art and sculptures he had throughout his home. "It must be so peaceful to live in a place that you don't have to have cameras just to try to catch your fucking neighbors," she huffed.

"Oh, it's very nice," he said. "I never really bring anyone out here, so I don't have any reason to. When I'm not home, I have someone house sit for me. And when I am home, I have all of the protection I need in my closet, so I have nothing to worry about. Cameras won't really do shit other than record a criminal, and what good is that going to fucking do me,"Brian asked.

"You don't get nervous being in this large condo by yourself without any kind of security, though," Tammy asked. "I have to keep my guys at home with me even when I am home because you never know what to expect."

"These guys around here respect me," he stated as he made them a drink. "I've lived here all of these years, and I've never had a problem, so I don't see one happening now."

He lit the fire in his fireplace, and the two laughed and joked about everything under the sun. Even though Brian wasn't the most attractive person to look at, he was definitely smart and could hold an exciting conversation.

After she had the chance to make them a few more drinks, and they both were feeling their liquor, Tammy walked over to his stereo to turn on some music.

"Brian let me tell you something about me," Tammy said as she began to dance to the smooth sounds that were flowing out of the speakers. "I'm a woman that loves to be in charge. Do you honestly think you can handle a woman like me that always feels the need to be in charge?"

Without saying a word, Brian nodded to let her know that her desire for power did not bother him at all.

"Excellent. Then be a good boy and wait for me in the bedroom. I'm going to go into the bathroom to freshen up and slip into something a little more comfortable. All I need you to do is be in the bedroom, naked, and waiting for me.

"Oh," she said before he left the room. "You better have the fucking condoms ready because I never let anyone in me raw," she ordered.

"Yes, ma'am," he answered back.

After several minutes, Tammy walked into his bedroom wearing only the red bottom heels that she had been wearing for the evening.

"I'm going to leave the music on, and you're going to be a good boy, and you are not going to talk for the rest of the evening," she instructed. "I'm going to dance for you, and the moment you lay one single finger on me, the show is over."

He nodded to let her know that he was willing to do whatever she wanted him to.

"Now, because I've been waiting for this moment longer than you have, I want to make sure that this night goes smoothly and without any issues. Normally I would trust you to be a good boy, but I don't want to give you a chance to let me down."

Tammy reached into her bag and grabbed two sets of handcuffs and a roll of pink duct tape. She straddled herself over him and placed her large breast in his face as she handcuffed his hands to the bed. She turned around and gently bounced on him while she handcuffed his feet to the footboard.

"Do you like that papi," she asked him seductively.

"Yes," he moaned out to her.

"Hmm, hmm, hmm," she said as she shook her head. "You've already broken one of my rules. I would hate to have to cut this good time short because of a three-letter word that you were not supposed to say at all," Tammy said. "I didn't want to have to use this, but since you clearly can't follow directions, I'm afraid I'm going to have to."

She removed a few pieces of the duct tape and placed them tightly over his lips.

She got up from the bed and dimmed the lights even lower than they already were. She continued to dance for him while she watched his dick get hard at the thought of finally being inside of her.

After dancing for a few moments, Tammy walked over to him and straddled him once more. She reached over to the nightstand and noticed that he had not followed her specific order of having the condoms ready.

"I swear I have to do everything myself," she said slightly irritably as she got up from the bed and went into her purse.

Brian could hardly contain the excitement of finally finding out what it felt like to be inside of Tammy that he began to squirm on the bed waiting on her to return.

Suddenly, the bedroom door flew open, and a tall man dressed in all black with a ski mask stood in the door's entrance.

Brian's eyes grew wide in surprise to see that he was lying there naked, handcuffed to a bed, with no way to protect him or Tammy.

Tammy pulled out her 9MM from her purse, placed one in the head, and pointed the gun directly at Brian.

"I have to admit," she started. "If I would have been some dumb broad, I really would have bought into this who charade of yours. The wining, dining, and gifts, the promises to make millions by putting me under your brand, if I was simple-minded, I really would have bought into this.

I realized a long time ago that you and I are in the exact same business. You really thought you had life fucked up to believe that you had any shot at my father's territory or money just for simply dealing with me. Let me tell you where your plan went wrong," Tammy continued as she walked over to him and placed the cold steel in between his legs. "You left your e-mail open one day, and I saw it all. Your fool-proof plan failed because it was planned by a damn fool," Tammy chuckled.

"You keep all of your passwords the same, and your every move is predictable. You're really not very good for someone who has been doing this so long. You think just because your clients are rich doctors, lawyers, actors, or congressmen, you were going to be exempt from the rules of this game?" She turned her attention over to the masked man.

"The guns and money are in the closet. I've written the combination inside the box of condoms." She walked over to the top of the bed, never once removing her gun from his sweaty body. "Now be a good boy and tell me where the product is," she asked as she ripped the duct tape from his lips."

"I'll let you kill me before I just let you take my shit," he responded with disgust.

"Now, you should know better than that. I wouldn't let you go that easily," Tammy said with a titter. "I know this is your stash house, so I'll tear this bitch up tile by tile and search every crease and crevice of this fucking house if I have to.

But see, we don't have that kinda time. I have three men parked outside of your mother's house in Dorchester. I know that your mother, wife, and four children are inside enjoying dinner as we speak."

Brian's eyes grew wide at the thought of his family being in harm's way.

"So we can do this the easy way, or we can do this the hard way, but I am not leaving without what the fuck I came here for. I'm going to ask you one more time. Where the fuck is the product" Tammy asked.

"The coke is in the guest bedroom next to the bathroom upstairs, and the weed is in the bathroom closet.

I'm going to get you back for this bit-," Brian said before Tammy used the butt of the gun to split open his lip.

Tammy quickly got dressed, and with the help of three of Tammy's other men and a few trips from the house to the car, they quickly collected what they were after and took off.

***

"Oh my gosh," Tammy screamed as she pulled at his clothes once they were safe inside their hotel room. "Is it bad that what we just did turns me on," she asked him with a giggle.

"Does it feel right," Patrick asked while he tried to take off his ski mask.

Tammy swatted his hands and fixed it back on his face. "It feels great. I feel alive," she exclaimed.

"You surprised the hell out of me," he laughed. "If I wouldn't have known better, I would have been scared that you had people in front of my house for real. That was very believable."

"Well, I wasn't going to leave without what I came for. My dad left me money to take care of myself in a few years, but in the meantime, I still have employees that need to eat and bills that have to be paid. All I want now is for you to fuck me while only wearing that ski mask," she demanded.

"Mi a bad man", he replied firmly. "You do what I say. Now, bend over," Patrick demanded.

Just as Tammy was about to give in, she noticed Jason calling her cell phone. Initially, she ignored his incessant calls, but once he started calling Patrick's phone, they knew it was urgent.

"What nigga," Patrick yelled into the phone, obviously aggravated. "Can't we celebrate in peace?"

After a few moments of silence, Patrick became more relaxed as he actively listened to whatever Jason was saying.

"Here," he said, finally passing Tammy the phone. "You really want to take this."

"Ugh," she grunted as she took the phone from him. "What up?"

"Yo Tee, I got some news we've been waiting mad long for," Jason spoke eagerly into the phone. "You know I'm still down here in Florida taking care of that one lil' mission you set up, and I got a major tip on who might have popped your father."

Tammy sat up, anxious to hear more.

"Aight, so one of these niggas that is serving some of these small-time hustlers out here is connected to the person who killed him."

"Beast, slow down and tell me everything you know," Tammy demanded.

"Ok," he huffed as he relaxed a little bit. "Someone finally came through with not only a tip but proof of that woman who killed your dad."

"A broad killed my pops," Tammy questioned. "Why? Who is she? What did she gain from it?"

"I haven't been able to get all of that because I haven't been able to find her," he responded. "But I got a lead on the closest person to her."

"Good. Tell me more."

"Well, apparently, her son Kyle, who goes by the nickname K.Y, was the last nigga to see her out here," Jason stated. "So what do you want me to do, boss?"

"Start getting all your product from him. Find out who his largest customer is and quadruple what you get from him. Make that nigga depend on our bread. Get in cool with him, and I'm going to figure out the rest of the game plan," Tammy responded.

"Are you sure you're ready for something like this, Tee? Revenge is a whole new kinda ball game. I know you to be a lot of things, but a killa ain't one," Jason asked.

"Just do what I said," Tammy said firmly as she lit her blunt and rolled back in the bed. "I've charged a lot of shit to this game, but somebody is going to pay for the death of my father."

| 18 |

Charge it to the Game 3: Three Sides to Every Story

He wasn't sure if it was the large amount of alcohol he drank, the fact that he couldn't stop reliving the sweet memories in his head, or the fact that over a year later, his heart still refused to mend, but he was determined to get his revenge that night. K.Y had dreamt about this moment every night for over 365 days.

With the help of Isabella and Josie, K.Y was finally successful in finding out Tammy and Patrick's whereabouts, and he knew he could not let this opportunity escape him.

"That bitch thought she would just get rich off of me and my shit," he thought as he stuffed his blue backpack with an array of guns and ammo.

"That motherfucker really thought he could fuck the woman I loved and live good off of my hard-earned money." Kyle huffed as he became angrier as the sight flashed through his mind of Patrick Bennett enjoying the life that K.Y. had worked so hard to have with Tamia Santiago, the only woman he had ever given his heart to.

He threw the backpack in the trunk of the rental, plugged the address in the GPS, and threw on some music as he sped off in search of his destination.

After driving close to an hour, he finally pulled up in front of a place he knew all too well. It caused his heart to fall further into his stomach than it had ever been when his nightmare had been confirmed. Tammy had brought Patrick to the exact same bungalow that she had brought him to. The same place where she had opened up and exposed her softer, more vulnerable side to him for the first time, she was now here doing it with another man.

K.Y. thought back to how Tammy made him feel like a king the last time he was there with her. She cooked for him and catered to his every need without him even having to ask. He had been sore and achy from the brutal beating he had received in front of Jason's studio in Orlando, FL, and she insisted that they get away so that he could relax. The pain he had felt that day didn't even come close to the torture he was feeling at that exact moment.

Then, the realization set in that she was probably the one who arranged the merciless beating he had received and only catered to his needs in an effort to salvage her guilt.

He made sure to be as quiet as possible as he retrieved the bag he had out of the trunk. He followed the trail that went to the bungalow's entrance.

He stood behind one of the large bushes that was closest to the door and used the large window a few feet away to his full advantage.

He watched on in agony as he observed Tammy sashay from the kitchen to the dining room in the Victoria Secret lingerie he had purchased for her as a gift when they had moved into their condo when they were still together.

He watched Patrick stare at the feast sitting in front of him. Through the cracked window, the sweet smell of Tammy's home cooking swayed through his nose and reminded him of yet another thing he missed about her. That woman could throw down in the kitchen.

Tammy briefly said grace over the meal, and they both sat down to enjoy the massive feast she had prepared.

K.Y. tried to look away from the seemingly happy couple as they ate, talked, and laughed. Still, even after the hurt, anguish, and pain she had caused him, everything about Tammy was beautiful, breathtaking, and hypnotizing.

After what felt like forever, Tammy got up from the table and cleared away all of the dishes. K.Y watched as Patrick pulled a blunt off the kitchen table, opened the door the led to the outside patio, and stepped outside in the direction of the beach.

Once Tammy was done cleaning up, she went into the room and resided there for a few moments. K.Y. knew that this was going to be his only opportunity to catch Patrick alone and slipping.

He slid a gun out of his bag and threw the backpack on. Then, he quietly made his way to where Patrick was.

He was able to use the loud sounds of the ocean to his advantage since Patrick never noticed him as he moved with much determination to finally receive revenge on his enemy.

The night was dark, and K.Y relied on the lights from the stars and the moon above as he finally stood in the presence of the man he had grown to hate with an immense passion.

He snuck up behind him, placed the gun to his temple, and placed a bullet in the head of the gun.

Patrick's demeanor never changed despite the cold steel that was unsuspectingly placed to the soft part of his skull. He continued to smoke his blunt as if he were unfazed.

"Nice to finally meet you motherfucker," K.Y stated through clenched teeth as he tried to remain quiet, so he didn't alarm Tammy. "You really thought you were going to break into my home, fuck my girl, take my shit, and live happily ever after," K.Y. asked him angrily.

K.Y. was thrown off guard by Patrick's nonchalant demeanor. Instead of begging for his life, like K.Y had hoped for, Patrick fell into a fit of evil laughter.

"Pull the trigger then motherfucker. You can't kill what's already dead, and I been gone," he said as he exhaled the smoke his lungs had been holding in.

"Anyway nigga, I know my queen taught you that you can't trip on what was never yours to begin with," Patrick said as his laughter roared again.

K.Y. didn't know what to do next. He didn't come with any other plan since Tammy had told him that over-planning something is the quickest way to ruin a plan.

He had envisioned killing Patrick many times before, but he wanted to see him squirm first. He wanted to inflict him with as much pain as he had a hand in causing.

"Kyle Cole," Tammy shrieked from behind him. "What the fuck are you doing?"

K.Y. didn't immediately turn around because he wasn't ready to face her yet. He could tell from the cracks in her voice as she spoke, he had already caused her a great deal of pain. Truthfully, he wanted his revenge, but he wanted her more.

He slowly turned his head and saw something he had never imagined in all of his time dreaming of this moment. He stared down the barrel of what he knew was a loaded gun being held by a dangerous woman.

ABOUT THE AUTHOR

Keaidy Bennett is an accomplished author, entrepreneur, and advocate for marginalized writers. As the owner of LexxiKhan Presents Publishing, a renowned publishing company, she is committed to empowering aspiring authors to find their authentic voice and share their unique stories with the world.

Keaidy's dedication to storytelling goes beyond the written word. She is currently in the process of turning her book Charge it to the Game into a television series. This transformative project not only brings her narrative to life on screen but also creates new jobs and opportunities for Afro-Latino creators and actors. For more information about the upcoming series, please visit ChargeItToTheGameSeries.com.

Keaidy was born in Honduras but presently resides in Orlando, Florida, with her three children. Through her work and her publish- ing company, she strives to make a lasting impact by championing diversity, authenticity, and inclusivity in literature.

To connect with Keaidy Bennett and stay updated on her latest projects, visit her website at www.lexxikhanpresents.com/kdboriginal

Keaidy loves hearing from her readers! Be sure to send her a text today! **407-890-8882.** Follow Keaidy on Instagram **@akawords** Follow the Charge it to the Game series on Instagram **@chargeittothegameseries**

Made in United States
North Haven, CT
29 October 2024

59599000R00088